Sexy Pleasures

Sexy Stories Collection

VOLUME 16

12 EROTIC SHORT STORIES

PORTIS NEWMAN

Publisher's Note: This is a work of fiction. Names,
characters, places, and incidents are a product of
the author's imagination. Locales and public
names are sometimes used for atmospheric
purposes. Any resemblance to actual people, living
or dead, or to businesses, companies, events,
institutions, or locales is completely coincidental.

Sexy Pleasures/ Portis Newman. -- 1st ed.
Xplicit Press, an imprint of TLM Media LLC

ISBN-13: 978-1-62327-547-1
ISBN-10: 1-62327-547-4
eISBN: 978-1-62327-597-6

Printed in the United States of America

CONTENTS

1 WORKING OVERTIME

Yvette's wet, sinful tongue slithered across the tip of her boss's pulsating dick slowly before taking him deep into her mouth. Her whimpering moans were muffled by the girth of Buck's scrumptious meat. She moved her lips ever so slowly, teasing and tantalizing her boss as she had every day since she started working for him.

She had thought about the repercussions the very first time that he had seduced her. Yvette was hooked the moment she felt his raging shaft slide into her bare, juicy slit for the first time. She didn't care that he was married. She didn't care that she was engaged or that Buck was nearly twenty years older than she was. Buck Graham knew how to please a woman and knew how to teach her to please him back.

The twenty-eight-year-old Hispanic secretary slid her hand slowly down the front of her skirt and caressed her smooth creamy thighs. Her slender fingers squeezed her supple flesh as they worked their way up to her hot, simmering quim. Her round, soft breasts rose and fell, straining to burst from her blouse with each deepening breath she took. Yvette was in heaven and wished the moment would last forever.

Suddenly the phone on her desk rang and jarred her away from her lurid fantasy. She frowned and picked up the phone. By the time she was done booking a client meeting for her boss, Yvette was trembling. She looked around quickly to see if anyone had noticed her moment of heat.

Seeing the coast was clear, she made a beeline for the restrooms. She quickly checked the stalls and to her relief, she was alone. Yvette splashed some cold water on her face and stared at herself in the mirror.

"Get it together, woman," she whispered as she noticed how her achingly hard nipples pressed through the sheer fabric of her blouse.

No, she had never actually had sex with Mr. Graham, but she obsessed over it constantly. From the moment she met him during her job interview all the way up until a few minutes ago, she fantasized about him having his way with her, every day, anywhere he wanted, no matter who was around. But today she went too far. Someone could have easily walked around the corner and caught her with her hand stuffed into her dripping panties.

Usually she'd take a nice, soothing shower, get dressed up in her sexiest lingerie, and then crawl into bed to fantasize. Yvette knew she was taking this well beyond a seemingly innocent crush. She had picked out lingerie to wear specifically for when she was with him in her mind. She even bought a big, ribbed dildo that she called "Buck" after him.

Something needed to give. Either she needed to drop it or have him fuck the infatuation out of her. She would have preferred the latter but knew that the former was the most likely to happen. Still, she held out hope. Anything could happen, right?

That night, Yvette took all of her naughty lingerie and "Buck" and packed them up in a box. She stowed the box in the furthest corner she could clear in her closet and closed the door. She stared at the door then suddenly giggled.

"The Buck stops here," she burst out laughing.

Her laughing died quickly, leaving her just staring at the door again. She needed to get out of her apartment so she called Daniel, her fiancé, and asked if he wanted to go out to eat. Not long after she was off the phone with him, she was dolled up and ready to go.

"What's wrong?" Daniel asked after she closed the door behind them.

"Just a long day is all," she said tiredly.

He took her hand and kissed the back of it. He always smiled when he saw the ring on her finger. Six more months and his dream would be fulfilled and they'd be husband and wife. Daniel thought she was the most amazing woman he had ever met. Yvette was his angel.

She was vivacious and so full of life. Dinner was nice. They went to a quiet little Italian restaurant near Daniel's neighborhood. Afterwards, they went back to his house and made love for hours. Yvette had never felt such passion with Daniel than she had that night. For once in the last six months, she had loved him without fantasizing about her boss.

The rest of the week breezed by for Yvette. Her weekend was spent with her fiancé and some friends planning various parts of their wedding. Not once did Buck ever enter her thoughts or dreams. Yvette was never happier. It was as if a great weight was lifted from her shoulders, and she could really be free and not feel bad for her obsession.

On Monday, Yvette received an e-mail from Mr. Graham regarding an appointment for an after-hour meeting. She wasn't surprised. He frequently stayed late or met with his engineers at a restaurant or bar to talk shop. She had been invited many times but this time it was only her on the appointment list and the meeting was to be held at his home.

During the course of the week, she was fantasy-free. In fact, she spent an unusually great amount of time with her fiancé. Buck was the furthest thing in her mind. It seemed she was over him, finally, which was good. If she hadn't dug down deep to find the resolve she needed, she would have ended up in a much worse situation than now. Finally, Friday came and with it, the appointment with Buck.

"Hi, you must be Yvette," said the woman who greeted her at the door. "I'm Dottie, Buck's wife."

"It's a pleasure," she replied after being welcomed into her boss' house.

The two-story Victorian was as lavish on the inside as it was on the outside. She couldn't help but feel poor when she looked at the expensive artwork on the walls and a myriad of exquisite vases that decorated the main living room. Dottie took her coat and hung it up in the closet before disappearing into the kitchen.

"Buck's running a little late," Dottie hollered. "Something to drink?"

"Sure," Yvette hollered back.

Her eyes turned to Buck's wife as she emerged from the kitchen with two glasses of wine. Yvette was a bit disappointed. She thought it would just be her and her boss tonight for their meeting. She had had dozens of very satisfying orgasms fantasizing about this very night from the day Buck asked her to his home for their little conference.

But Dottie threw a very curvaceous wrench into her sinful plans. She could see why Buck never gave her a second glance. Dottie was straight up hot. Yvette didn't know what her exact age was but knew she was only a couple of years younger than her husband. When Dottie apologized for looking frightful, Yvette almost choked on her wine.

Dottie was far from frightful. She wore a very figure-flattering off-white dress that dipped deeply at the neck, exposing the deep, cavernous cleavage between her breasts. Yvette thought hers were large at 35DD, but Dottie's had to be at least 38's or maybe even 40's. She had a slender frame with delicious curves in all the right places. Dottie's body made her breasts look even bigger than they really were.

"How old are you?" Yvette asked.

"I'll be 45 in a few months," Dottie answered with a proud smile.

"Wow! I hope I look as good as you do when I'm 45," Yvette said.

Dottie gave her a sweet smile. She prided herself on her looks at her age. She worked hard to keep her slim figure, and Buck appreciated every subtle curve of her body. Dottie gave Yvette's hand a squeeze and thanked her for the compliment. They turned to the door as Buck finally found his way home.

"Well it's about time, darling," Dottie said, meeting her husband near the door and giving him a series of gentle kisses.

"Sorry," he said as he hung up his coat. "One of the engineers needed me to go over some blueprints with him. I swear that contract is going to leech us dry."

"Give me a moment, okay?" Buck said to Yvette then disappeared down the hall.

Dottie smiled at their guest and followed her husband.

In the bedroom, Buck was trading his business suit for a loose T-shirt and jeans. His wife slid against him and kissed him deeply, pressing her elegant body against him firmly. Their moist tongues danced together slowly while Dottie's hands roamed over her husband's muscled back.

"She's pretty," Dottie whispered in his ear. "I want her."

Dottie smiled at the slight shock on her husband's face then slowly slid to her knees. She pulled out his flaccid cock and kissed its head. It slowly sprung to life under her sensuous attention. She moaned into Buck's dick as she sucked on it, feeling it hardening to full length inside of her mouth. Dottie loved the feeling of her husband's large cock as it hardened in her warm, wet mouth.

"Maybe," Buck whispered as he closed his eyes to enjoy his wife's sucking.

"Tell me you wouldn't fuck her if you had the chance," Dottie cooed before sinking his engorged shaft into her mouth again.

"Yessss," he hissed when he felt the head of his throbbing meat press against the back of his wife's throat.

In no time Dottie and her sinfully expert mouth had Buck toeing the line of climax. She sounded like a freight train, breathing heavily through her nostrils as she sucked for dear life. Buck's hips pumped his pulsing shaft in and out of his wife's hot, wet mouth fervently. He felt his balls tightening and knew it was a matter of moments before he'd shoot his wad down her throat.

Dottie pumped his cock with her fist as she swallowed it over and over again, cooing and whimpering for him to blast her mouth with his hot, thick cum. Buck started to grunt quietly, not wanting to tip Yvette off to his wife's sinful pleasuring. Dottie's lips glided over his saliva-lubed shaft then felt his flesh swell as he was about to explode.

Buck's salty jizz erupted in her mouth. She moaned on his dick as stream after naughty stream pumped into her mouth and oozed down her throat. Dottie milked every ounce of his delicious seed she could then let his softening rod slide from her mouth. Normally, she would have let some of his cum splatter on her face then smear it around with his throbbing glans, but she didn't feel like having to clean herself up and redo her makeup for Yvette, though she'd be interested to see how that young, sexy, Mexican morsel would have reacted.

Meanwhile, Yvette was waiting patiently in the living room. She fiddled with the hem of her skirt and wondered if she had dressed inappropriately. Her black skirt was short, barely covering half of her toned, caramel thighs with a tiny slit up one side. Its stretchy fabric hugged her hips and ass and would have easily shown her panty line if she hadn't been wearing a thong. Her jade, button-up top wasn't exactly businesslike, but it was better than the tank top she had considered. She thought one too many buttons had been left unclasped, but despite her feeling to cover her chest a little more, she left it as it was.

She huffed quietly and began to think about Buck again. Being in his house was genuinely erotic and the idea that his bedroom was just a dozen feet down the hall made her being there that much more exciting. She wondered how it would be decorated but slipped into a naughty thought.

She imagined chains dangling from the ceiling, cuffed to her wrists, imprisoning her there in all her glorious nudity. Buck was pounding his hips into her voluptuous ass as he fucked her mindlessly while she was helpless to stop him. That's exactly what she wanted. She wanted him to treat her like a mindless slab of meat and fuck her until she collapsed from exhaustion.

Buck and Dottie watched her quietly from the shadow of the hallway. Yvette's eyes were closed and her hands caressed the outsides of breasts through her blouse. Her creamy, smooth thighs gently rubbed together, each caressing the other while she was lost in her fantasy. They were entranced by her.

Buck slid his arms around his wife and pulled her against him. She could feel the growing bulge in his jeans press against her silky smooth ass. She took his hand and cupped it over her breast with a squeeze. Dottie massaged her round tit with her husband's hand, mimicking Yvette's own self-pleasuring.

In her fantasy, Yvette was moaning for her boss to fuck her harder. Buck did. He reached around and grabbed her large, bouncing tits and fondled them. Her erect nipples shot spikes of pleasure throughout her body when Buck squeezed them between his fingers as he pounded her dripping pussy relentlessly.

"I really, really want her," Dottie whispered. "She's absolutely gorgeous."

"She has a great body," Buck whispered back while nibbling on his wife's neck.

"She's fantasizing about you," his wife said and ground her tender ass playfully against his crotch.

"How do you know?" he asked.

"You didn't see the look in her eyes when you came in," Dottie turned around and kissed him gently on the lips. "And she's feeling herself up in our home."

Buck smiled and looked over his wife's shoulder. Yvette had her legs parted slightly now. Her slender fingers danced along her thigh and teased the edge of her white panties. Her forehead was slightly wrinkled in concentration, while her other hand was inside her bra, massaging her magnificent breast.

"Want me to run interference for you baby?" Dottie kissed her husband on the tip of the nose and gave him a loving pat on the ass.

He smiled but swallowed hard. He never thought of bringing another woman from work into their sexy, sinful circle. They've had other women before, just never from either of their workplaces. In fact, there are times where it seemed Dottie enjoyed being with another woman than he did. He always thought she should have been born a man because she was nothing more than an oversexed pig on some days. This appeared to be one of those days.

Without another word, Dottie kissed Buck deeply on the lips then smoothed her dress out before appearing from the hallway. Yvette was oblivious to Dottie's presence while she continued her fantasy. Dottie's mouth watered as she watched Yvette rub her fingers slowly up and down the gentle crease in her panties. Her panties were moistening with a very visible wet spot beneath her fingers.

Yvette opened her eyes, suddenly having the feeling someone was watching her. Her eyes shot wide open as she saw Dottie standing in front of her. She hiked down her skirt and tried to button up her blouse quickly. Yvette could feel the heat of embarrassment in her cheeks.

"I'm so sorry," she told Buck's wife.

"That's okay," the older woman said as she slid onto the couch beside her husband's employee.

"No, no it's not. I better leave," Yvette said and started to stand.

"Shhhh," Dottie whispered and put her hand on her shoulder, telling her it really was okay.

"You should never feel sorry for indulging in pleasure, dear," Dottie told her.

Yvette watched the woman timidly. She trembled inside from getting caught in one of her fantasies. Getting caught didn't disturb her as much as having the fantasy. So far, she had been a good girl. She hadn't had a fantasy about Buck in a while and was upset that she succumbed to her desire and in her boss' house no less.

"Really?" Yvette whispered, very aware of Dottie's hand petting her knee.

"It's okay that you want my husband," Buck's wife said softly. "Like it's okay that I want you."

Yvette sat in mild shock. She could tell by the looks that Dottie gave her that the older woman was attracted to her but had no idea that she would actually act on her want. She closed her eyes and felt Dottie's lips brush against hers.

Buck watched quietly from the hallway. He stroked his massive cock back to life while he watched his wife seduce Yvette. He was amazed how Dottie was always able to conquer another woman despite any reservations her victim may have had. Sensual seduction was one of the qualities he loved most in his wife, though their bond went deeper than that.

He rubbed this thumb over his pulsing glans with each determined stroke. He watched as his wife tenderly kissed Yvette at first. Their bodies gently writhed together as their kisses became deeper, more passionate. He could see their tongues slipping between each other's mouths. Buck loved watching the entire scene unfold before him.

Soon Dottie had Yvette lying on the couch. She kissed the young woman's smooth neck. Her lips brushed over her supple flesh as she suckled then nipped at her skin. With each kiss, Dottie moved lower. Her fingers deftly unbuttoned Yvette's blouse, exposing her deliciously large breasts framed by her thin, lacy bra. Buck's dick pumped, twitching several times as the hunger grew inside of him. He knew he'd get to join in soon.

Yvette's world spun around her. She had never imagined herself being with another woman. Somehow she thought it was wrong but there was something intoxicating in the way Dottie touched her. It was as if this woman held her in her heart and loved her like a mate instead of just some stranger she was attracted to. Yvette never had a feeling of doubt, only passion.

She moaned and arched her back with each gently touch on her body. Heated desire swarmed through her, urging her to give into Dottie more and more with each passing moment. The moment she felt the rush of cool air brush over her hot, dripping pussy when her soaked panties were peeled away, whatever reservations she had, however slight, drowned in a sea if bliss.

Buck watched his wife between Yvette's toned, creamy thighs expertly eating her succulent, bare pussy. The pressure inside of him was more than he could stand. He had to join in. With his raging shaft squeezed between his fingers, Buck appeared from hallway and joined them.

Yvette moaned softly while she kneaded her large, pillowing breasts. She dug in fingers gently into her flesh and teased her sensitive nipples. The feeling of Dottie's cool, wet tongue sliding deeply between her flaring, moist folds drove her absolutely insane. She had never felt such sinful delight in her life; then again, she had never had another woman feast on her hungry pussy before.

Suddenly she felt something brush across her lips. Her eyes opened lazily and Buck's beautiful cock loomed mere millimeters from her mouth. Yvette groaned and closed her eyes. She opened her mouth and accepted him inside of her.

Buck groaned as she started to suck him gently. Her fingers wrapped around his engorged shaft and stroked him gently. Her soft, stiff tongue circled the rim of his head as she sucked. Yvette was in heaven. She couldn't believe this was actually happening. As much as she loved the exquisite tongue fucking that Buck's wife was giving her, she couldn't wait to feel his stiff meat driving deep into her burning cunt.

The pressure was building inside of her, driving her mad with euphoria. Dottie's lips were wrapped around her sensitive nub as she tongued and sucked her hard clit. She sucked and stroked he boss' shaft harder while his wife drove her insane. She could feel her orgasm rushing at her like a runaway train. Soon it would crash and explode into a cloud of pure pleasure.

"Oh yes!" Yvette cried out. "There! There! Ohhhh! Lick my pussy harder!"

Yvette's hips moved wildly against Dottie's hot tongue. She held Buck's rock-hard dick in a death grip as she stroked him fast and feverishly. Closer her climax loomed, teasing her with the anticipation of exploding in complete satisfaction.

"I'm cumming! I'm cumming!" she moaned incoherently as the bliss overtook her body and threatened to burn her into oblivion.

Dottie sucked harder on Yvette's clit and pressed her fingers against her tight ass. Yvette arched her back and burst. The inferno of lust slowly burned through her from head to toe. Dottie had a hard time keeping up with her wild convulsions. Her entire body shook from the intense fire that wracked every nerve in her.

When it was over, her dreamy eyes glanced between her boss and his wife. Her large breasts rose and fell sharply with each labored breath. Her pussy burned with hunger and craved for more. She hoped there would be more. Yvette knew there would be more.

Dottie stripped naked in front of them. She gave her husband a deep, wet kiss as she crushed her hot tits into his smooth chest. Her fingers wrapped around his throbbing meat and stroked him lovingly. After she broke the kiss, she looked at Yvette and extended her hand.

Yvette took Dottie's hand and allowed herself to be helped off the couch. The older woman slid onto the couch and reclined back into the semi-smooth, fluffy cushions. She spread her legs slowly, revealing her glistening, smooth pussy to the young woman. Yvette felt her own pussy twinge and her mouth began to water as her eyes drank in every sensual curve of Dottie's body.

Buck took her by the shoulders firmly and eased her to the floor. Yvette crawled on top of Dottie and began kissing her hungrily. Their large breasts pressed together hotly as their tongues eagerly explored each other's mouth. She moaned into Dottie's mouth as the older woman caressed her back then began squeezing her young, tender ass.

Dottie's fingers dipped between Yvette's cheeks and spread them, opening the Latina up for her husband's pleasure. Buck wasted no time in taking advantage. He drew up behind Yvette and ran his swollen cockhead up and down between her dripping lips. Her juices glistened on his head, lubing it to slide into her easily.

Buck pressed his cock between her velvety folds and penetrated her tight snatch. Yvette grunted as her boss sank his entire length into her with one fluid thrust. Buck held still for a moment, enjoying the heat and wetness of her tight hole. Dottie slid up a bit on the couch and lifted her round, heavy breasts to Yvette's face.

Yvette dove on them eagerly, licking and kissing and sucking fervently, smearing her saliva all over the woman's succulent breasts. She sucked one of Dottie's hard, puckered nipples into her mouth and fed on it like a baby. Meanwhile, Buck was reaming the hell out of her burning, tight cunt.

Sweat ran down his face as he pumped his hips into her ravenously. Buck drilled his cock into her as fast and hard as he could. He couldn't remember the last time he had a woman with such a tight pussy. The pleasure that swept through Yvette's body made her delicious hole squeeze his angry shaft like a vice. He knew that he couldn't hold out very long amid the tightness that milked his throbbing dick.

They fucked wildly. Their sweaty, steaming bodies writhed together in single mass of pure, blatant sex. Yvette had two fingers shoved up Dottie's pussy as far as they would go. She loved the feeling of the woman's slick juices leaking down her hand and arm.

"Fuck her, baby!" Dottie moaned at her husband. "Fuck your dirty office slut!"

Yvette bucked her ass against her boss' thrusts, fucking her pussy against him with every ounce of energy her fatigued muscles could spare. Hearing the woman call her a slut made her feel even dirtier and sexier than she already did. Buck's cock dominated her wanton slit and pushed her closer to another orgasm.

She felt light-headed and thought she was going to pass out. Yvette nuzzled her face between Dottie's silky breasts and moaned as loud as she could. Both women could sense the other was getting closer to cumming, and as their moans rose in volume and pitch, Buck felt his balls starting to tighten again.

His secretary arched her back and shoved her ass against him hard as she came. Yvette wailed loudly and shoved a third finger into Dottie's slippery cunt. Dottie's nails dug into Yvette's back as she screamed through her climax. Their bodies jerked violently from the intense pleasure that seared through them.

"Here I come!" Buck groaned and pulled his enraged dick from his secretary's used pussy.

Both women scrambled to their knees and were met with a furious spray of his thick, nasty cum. Buck pumped his massive cock quickly as he steered spurt after glorious spurt of his salty juice onto their faces. Yvette didn't think he would ever stop cumming. Dottie was used to her husband giving her a nice, erotic cumbath.

When he was finally done, his wife and secretary had loads of cum oozing down their faces and dripping onto their heaving tits. Yvette swallowed the cum that had shot into her mouth. She moaned in satisfaction then spent a few moments licking Dottie's supple body clean of Buck's fluids. Dottie smiled and looked at the clock.

"My, it's getting late," she remarked. "I think you better stay for the night."

Yvette reached out and gave Buck's semi-flaccid cock a hearty squeeze and a soft kiss on its throbbing head.

"I'll stay for as long as you want this slutty little office fuck," she said with a wink.

2 MOVING IN

Starting Over

"Thank you so much!" Amber said before hanging up the phone.

She sighed with relief and smiled. Her brother, John, and his wife, Jeanette, had agreed to let her move in with them for a short time until she could get back on her feet. The last six months had been hell for the 23-year-old, out-of-work editorial assistant. Amber lost her job when the publishing house she worked for downsized considerably and work was hard to come by. She waited tables in the evening while she scoured the city for a new job.

Nearly three weeks ago, she received a phone call from her boss. He put in a good word for her with an associate that was the chief editor for a publisher in Amber's hometown. He said to expect a call later that afternoon and so she did. She talked for hours with Cindy, and afterwards, she was offered a job as an assistant editor. She happily took it before realizing that she had no means to move.

Her savings dwindled, and with no steady income, Amber had no way to put a deposit down on a simple studio apartment. Fortunately, her brother and his wife still lived there and offered to set her up in a spare room in their home until she had a few paychecks under her belt and get her own place. Amber and John were only about a year or so apart and had a very close relationship. Jeanette, on the other hand, was somewhat of a mystery to her.

Amber had only met her during the wedding, and once before when Amber went to visit before graduating college. She didn't spend much time with her sister-in-law, but Jeanette seemed to be looking forward to her living with them so they could get to know each other better. Amber was pretty excited about it, too.

Two weeks after moving in with her brother and sister-in-law, Amber finally got to start working again. She was up and gone before the other two had even stirred. She made sure her outfit was neatly pressed and her hair was pulled up in a tight, professional-looking bun. It made her look like a little like a librarian, the kind of sexy librarian that teenagers fantasized about.

Amber was very attractive. Her body had all the right curves in all the right places. John had commented several times on how similar she and his wife looked. It was almost like looking in a mirror. Funnier even was how Amber was only about two months older than Jeanette. They could have been sisters.

"Good morning, Amber," her new boss, Cindy Donnelly, greeted her.

"Good morning, Mrs. Donnelly," she said cheerfully.

"None of that 'missus' stuff here," Cindy said with a smile. "It makes me feel old. Just Cindy is fine."

Amber nodded and followed her boss to her office. After getting a run-down on the publishing house and some coworker introductions, Cindy took her to her new office. The office was quite beautiful. It was lavishly decorated and had a window. It wasn't at all like the office she had before. Amber knew she had a good thing here.

"On your desk is a stack of romance manuscripts," Cindy pointed out. "I need you to go through them today and pick out a few you think would make a decent sale."

"Sure thing, Cindy," Amber said excitedly.

"I'll warn you though," Cindy said with a big smile. "Most of it is trash. We get a lot of smut, you know, the kind of stuff you'd publish in a men's magazine. I don't mind racy, but it has to be tasteful, please."

Amber nodded and watched her boss leave. She settled in and started perusing through the manuscripts. After about the first ten, Amber had to agree with Cindy. Most of the storylines were great. There was a lot of passion and emotion, but the sex scenes were downright pornographic in some of them. Her head spun at how awful some of it was.

"He fucked her with his meaty cock, harder and deeper like he was drilling for oil?" She sat the manuscript down and just shook her head.

Amber was down for reading porn now and then, but the quality here was just laughable. She reached under her skirt and traced her lithe finger across the gentle indent over her quim. Dry as a bone. Amber realized that the kind of books they were looking for not only stimulated the reader's loins but also stimulated their minds and emotions, too. They wanted something the reader could connect with. So far, she hadn't found one.

With the clock nearing five, Amber looked at the dwindling stack and sighed. Maybe she wasn't cut out to screen romance novels. Maybe Cindy would have found at least a handful of hopefuls; so far, Amber had found zilch. Just when she thought it looked hopeless, Amber picked up the manuscript she had been looking for. It was nearly perfect.

As she read through it, she could feel the heat seeping into her like a sauna. Her breathing became shallow, and she caught herself massaging her breasts a few times. The passion of the story filled her with desire for the main character. Amber completely fell in love with the young woman's plight to be with the one she loved. Her heart ached with anticipation right up until she found out that the woman loved another woman.

That little fact sobered her quickly. Obviously, it was a very well written, emotional piece, but she just couldn't get past the main character being a lesbian. Why would such a woman pass up the rather hunky farmhand to be with the farmer's wife? It was dizzying to say the least. Amber pushed the manuscript aside with a bit of nervousness.

There was no way that she could toss it out as trash when in fact it was very good. Amber discovered that deep down the idea of a woman loving another woman disturbed her. It wasn't natural, and Amber wasn't sure if she could read any more, let alone edit it. So she sat there and gazed at the impasse before her. She picked it up and looked at it again.

"Just be professional," Amber told herself. "This is probably Cindy's idea of a test. Ace it and move to greener pastures."

"Well?" Cindy asked, completely startling Amber. She was so lost in thought that she hadn't seen her boss standing in front of her desk.

"This one is fabulous," Amber said with a smile. "The rest were pretty hopeless. There might be a project or two for a college student to work out but that's about it."

"Told ya," Cindy said and snatched the manuscript. "Let me have a look at it."

Of course, Amber didn't object. You just don't object to your boss exacting their will upon the situation. Never. She watched Cindy's expression as she read. She was like a statue. Nothing changed. No smile, no frown, no arch of an eyebrow, nothing. After the first chapter, Cindy laid the manuscript in her lap and looked at Amber dubiously.

"It's pretty good," Cindy remarked. "Even though it's about an obviously lesbian woman, it has passion and a real heartfelt story to it. The sex scenes probably need to be spruced up a bit, but it looks pretty polished."

Amber nodded. She hadn't gotten to the sex scenes yet, so she couldn't really comment on them. Cindy sat the manuscript on the desk and gave her a quirky little look before leaving. It was five, so Amber tucked the manuscript into her briefcase and headed home. If this work was to be her inaugural test, she was bent to passing it with flying colors.

When Amber walked in the door, she found a note sitting on the counter. Her brother and his wife had gone out to dinner and a movie. She smiled as she tossed the piece of paper in the trash. It would give her some time to curl up with the manuscript and give it some further reading. After a quick shower and bite to eat, Amber curled up on the couch and started to read.

Hours later, the sound of the front door closing jarred her awake. Amber stretched and glanced sleepily around. She hadn't realized how drained she was from a rather long day. She yawned and stretched, then smiled as she saw Jeanette walk by.

"Hey there, sleepyhead," Jeanette said cheerfully.

"Back already?" she asked.

"Honey, it's after nine," Jeanette pointed out as she hung her purse and coat on the rack.

"After nine?" Amber asked in surprise and looked at her watch. It wasn't just after nine, it was almost ten.

"Where's John?" Amber noticed her brother hadn't come home.

"Work," Jeanette frowned. "Something happened and he got called in. Something about a firewall or a system crash. Something technical that he needed to go in and fix."

Amber nodded. Her mind was still quite hazy from the nap and she decided to turn in. Jeanette understood and hoped that tomorrow they'd all get to sit down for a good home-cooked meal to catch up. They hadn't had much time to visit since Amber had moved in with them. Amber liked the idea and trudged off to bed.

Reading with Jeanette

Something woke Amber from her deep sleep. Her eyes suddenly opened, and she stared at the dim ceiling. She wasn't sure what woke her. Amber pulled the covers around her tightly and rolled onto her side. She listened for a little bit more before closing her eyes.

There it was again. She opened her eyes and breathed shallowly to concentrate. Amber couldn't hear clearly enough, but whatever it was sounded like, it was coming from John and Jeanette's room. As she focused, she heard it more clearly. It sounded like a gasp.

She wondered if everything was okay. She didn't hear John come home, but then again, she was dead to the world, and a dump truck could have torn through the house and she wouldn't have noticed. Amber decided to investigate.

She slid out of bed and slipped her silk robe on to cover her naked body. Amber moved a lot when she slept and found that even her bra and panties would become unbearably uncomfortable by the end of the night; she had learned that sleeping in the buff, on the other hand, was tremendously comfortable.

Amber crept down the tiny hall to her brother's bedroom. She stood outside and listened for a moment. The door was cracked and she resisted the urge to look. She wasn't sure if she could recover from seeing her brother and his wife making love, but the sounds deeply concerned her. Hopefully, if she did see them in the act, they'd be under the blankets enough to shield her from any uncomfortable glimpses.

She shifted her feet quietly and decided to peek anyway. If there was something wrong, she'd never forgive herself for being this close and not checking on them. As she peered into the bedroom, she was met with the most shocking sight she had ever seen in her short lifetime. She looked away quickly in embarrassment.

John wasn't home yet it seemed, and she caught an eyeful of her sister-in-law's naked body. She seemed to be masturbating while reading something. Amber recalled the scene for a moment, and then she remembered the manuscript. Where had she put it? Was that what Jeanette was reading? She hadn't paid much attention to it at first. She peeked in to see again.

It was. Jeanette held the manuscript in one hand and was gently massaging her breasts with the other. Her hand left her body just long enough to flip a page. Her nipples were hard, and her fingers rubbed them urgently. Her hips moved gently as if begging for someone to touch her bare, exposed quim. Amber watched her in amazement.

For a moment, she felt bad about spying on her sister-in-law. But the sight of Jeanette touching herself while reading the manuscript was intoxicating. Amber couldn't decide whether it was the thought of the story being so provocative to move Jeanette to masturbate while reading it, or if it was the idea of watching her do it.

Suddenly, Amber became very self-conscious. She wondered what Jeanette must think of her for bringing that kind of novel home to work on. The damage was done, but she still felt an overwhelming urge to get that manuscript back. She stepped back from the door, and her eyes searched all over for an answer of how to do just that.

She went back to her room and poked her head out as if she had journeyed down the hall. She steadied herself by taking a deep breath.

"Jeanette?" she called out down the hall. She waited for a moment, but there was no reply.

"Jeanette?" she asked a little louder as she left her room and walked halfway down the hall.

"I'm in here," Jeanette hollered from her bedroom. Amber crept closer to her sister-in-law's door.

"Are you still up?" Amber asked quietly from just outside the door.

"Yeah," Jeanette answered and told her to come in.

Amber took a deep breath and slowly opened the door. When she walked in, there was Jeanette lying under her covers, completely covered up with the manuscript in hand. Jeanette lowered her reading glasses a little and smiled.

"You know, this is pretty good," Jeanette said and waved the stack of papers. "I hope you don't mind. I couldn't sleep and was sorta curious about your work."

"I haven't read very far," Amber

admitted. "I usually only read the first chapter or so to screen each piece to decide if it would be a candidate for further examination."

"Oh, then you have to read more," Jeanette said.

She moved the covers a bit so Amber could join her. Amber hesitated for a moment then decided that there would be no harm in just reading a little. If anything, she could fake getting sleepy and leave at a moment's notice.

Amber slid under the covers with Jeanette. She nuzzled in next to her and the two started to read the manuscript together. Jeanette gave her a quick rundown of what had happened up to the point she was at. Amber was quite aware that Jeanette was still naked under the blankets. She probably didn't have the time to slip something on when I called out to her, Amber thought.

As they read, Amber would glance down, catch a glimpse of Jeanette's breast, and still-hard nipple in the shadows under the covers. Reality was beginning to slide toward the surreal. There she was, lying in bed with her sister-in-law, who was naked, all she had on was a silk robe to cover her own naked body, and they were reading a romance novel about a lesbian. It really wasn't the most optimal situation for her to be in. Besides, the novel was rather inviting, and she could feel its effects starting to seep into her body.

"Here," Jeanette said as she handed Amber the manuscript. "Arm's getting a little tired."

Amber smiled and took the manuscript with a nod. Jeanette rolled onto her side and snuggled a little closer with her. She could faintly smell her sister-in-laws arousal. Whether the soft, musky scent was still lingering from her earlier masturbation or further reading had renewed her excitement, it was still there.

As they continued to read, Jeanette laid her head on Amber's shoulder and slid her arm over her midsection. Amber stifled a groan at the touch of Jeanette's bare breasts on her arm. Between the book and her hot, young, naked sister-in-law pressed against her, Amber was starting to lose her mind. As the story continued, she started to replace the images of the characters in her head with her and Jeanette.

Embracing Her Sister-In-Law

"Kinda makes you wet, doesn't it?" Jeanette asked softly.

"Huh?" Amber feigned. She wasn't sure if she wanted to go down that road or not. A part of her did, but a part of her reminded herself that this was her brother's wife.

"I asked if the story makes you wet," Jeanette purred.

Jeanette took Amber's hand and moved it between her creamy soft thighs. Amber inhaled sharply as her sister-in-law moved her hand to her drenched pussy. Everything inside of her begged for her to leave but she couldn't. She was paralyzed and forced to endure Jeanette's cravings.

Jeanette ran Amber's hand over her dripping lips. Amber groaned softly and turned her head to look at her sister-in-law. Jeanette's eyes were closed and her lips were parted slightly as she cooed at the pleasure. Amber watched her for a moment then her eyes opened. Jeanette smiled.

"See how wet I am?" Jeanette asked her.

"Yes," Amber replied quietly.

"I bet you are wet, too," Jeanette whispered.

Amber was sure she was. If she wasn't already wet from reading the steamy manuscript, then petting Jeanette's dripping cunt surely got her juices flowing. Amber tried to answer her sister-in-law, but the sounds wouldn't come. As hard as she tried, she couldn't. Jeanette leaned forward and kissed her on the tip of the nose.

"May I see?" Jeanette asked quietly.

Amber couldn't answer. Her body was starting to heat up and her breathing had become shallow as she started to consciously rub Jeanette's pussy. Jeanette waited a bit before asking again, and when she did, Amber simply closed her eyes and nodded. She took a deep breath and waited to be touched.

She felt Jeanette's hand slip under her robe and caress her thigh gently. As she slowly parted her legs, her sister-in-law moaned softly. Amber wondered if she had ever been with a woman before. She didn't know. She didn't know much about the young woman whose hand was slowly creeping up her thigh. When Jeanette's fingers brushed her pussy, Amber moaned innocently.

The sensation sent sparks of pleasure throughout her body. She had never been touched so intimately by a woman before. Amber struggled inside. Should she stop Jeanette now before things went too far or allow herself to be seduced? The moment Jeanette's fingers found her aching clit, the desire that welled deeply inside her made the decision for her.

Amber's moans came softly with each tender stroke of her engorged nub. She tried to mirror Jeanette's movement and rubbed her sister-in-law's clit gently. Both women were slowly giving into the fantasy called forth by the sinful manuscript. Their eyes were closed and their cooing filled the small bedroom.

"Jeanette," Amber moaned softly.

She turned to look at her sister-in-law and then kissed her gently. Their lips brushed together hesitantly. The sparks of passion ignited into full-out desire at the first touch. They began to kiss gently but determinedly. Amber parted her lips and slid her tongue timidly into Jeanette's mouth.

Amber's tongue searched eagerly for Jeanette's. She felt empowered by the feeling of being with another woman and rolled on top of her sister-in-law. She felt the slick wetness from Jeanette's dripping pussy against her thigh. As they kissed, Jeanette moved her hips gently and ground her needy slit into her leg.

Amber did the same. She humped Jeanette's thigh slowly. Each time her sensitive clit rubbed along her sister-in-laws supple flesh, she moaned. She lowered herself even more until their soft breasts touched. Jeanette put her arms around Amber and pulled her down harder. Their pillowy breasts mashed together and their hard nipples poked and prodded at each other.

The two women kissed more hungrily now. A mixture of their saliva ran down Jeanette's cheek and chin as their tongues swirled furiously. Amber felt so sexy, so alive; she didn't want it to end. All sorts of naughty thoughts swirled through her mind as she planned her next move. Jeanette may have started the whole encounter, but Amber was sure to direct the action from here on out.

Amber broke their kiss and traced her lips along Jeanette's jaw to her neck. Her sister-in-law moaned wantonly as she traced her tongue along Jeanette's neck to her ear. She sucked on her earlobe gently as she ground her thigh into the woman's slick pussy. Their bodies writhed gently on the bed as she continued to pleasure her sister-in-law.

Amber felt the pressure building inside as the passion and desire mounted. She knew she'd climax soon, but she had other plans before then. Amber slowly kissed her way down Jeanette's body. Her sinful tongue lapped at a hard nipple before she sucked it between her lips. Jeanette moaned and arched her back, pressing her soft breast against Amber's mouth.

Her sister-in-law's reaction invigorated her. She felt powerful and sexy as she engaged in their taboo sex. Jeanette's silky breast felt extremely erotic pressing against her mouth and cheeks and Amber sucked harder. She flicked her tongue and swirled it around Jeanette's erect nipple hungrily. A gentle nip with her teeth sent a shudder through Jeanette.

Finally, Amber threw off the sheets and shed her untied robe. The lust in

Jeanette's eyes was overwhelming. She had never had anyone look at her with such desire and made her feel very sexy. Jeanette arched her back and lifted her arms over her head as she slowly spread her legs and offered her succulent pussy to Amber.

Amber lowered her face to Jeanette's quivery slit. She used her fingers to gently spread her sister-in-law's juicy lips. Her body trembled in fear, excitement, and anticipation. She gazed at Jeanette's clean-shaven pussy and felt her mouth start to water. It was beautiful and her clit was protruding slightly from beneath its hood. There were so many places to start that Amber wondered if Jeanette thought she was getting cold feet as she just knelt there, staring.

She threw caution to the wind. They had come this far, they may as well go all the way. Amber ran her tongue deeply between Jeanette's open folds. The taste was new and inviting. Amber wanted more. She licked her tongue deeply through her sister-in-law's dripping pussy recklessly. A thirst built up inside her and the more she lapped the closer she came to quenching it.

Jeanette arched her back and howled like an animal. Her breasts heaved with each frenzied gulp of air, and her fingers pulled and twisted her hard nipples gently. Amber mashed her face between Jeanette's legs harder. She had no idea what she was doing, but by the sound of the other young woman's moans, she was doing something right.

Then something clicked in Amber's head. She closed her eyes while stabbing her tongue deep into Jeanette's slimy cunt. She thought about how she masturbated. She pictured herself touching her own body and what made her squirm and what drove her to delightful heights. Then she pictured Jeanette doing all of those sinful things to her and used it as a roadmap to her sister-in-law's climax.

Amber replaced her tongue with two fingers and circled her lips around Jeanette's throbbing clit. She immediately felt the tightness squeeze her fingers as she slid them and out slowly, twisting and stirring at the same time. Jeanette nearly sat up at the intense pleasure when Amber began sucking her clit.

Faster, Amber fucked Jeanette with her fingers, adding a third to her burning hole. Her sister-in-law moved her hips wildly, and Amber had a hard time keeping her mouth and tongue firmly planted on her sensitive clit. Finally, Amber felt Jeanette wrap her arms around the back of her head and pull her as hard as she could against her screaming pussy.

Amber moaned in delight as her sister-in-law fucked her face hard and fast. She knew that Jeanette was nearing her orgasm and would soon tumble into an abyss of blinding pleasure. Suddenly, Jeanette lifted her ass completely off the bed as she bucked her hips wildly.

"Fuck me, Amber!" Jeanette cried. "Yes! Yes! I'm cumming!"

A burst of warm juices hit Amber's face like a sledgehammer as Jeanette reached her orgasm. Amber ate Jeanette's spasming pussy like a schoolboy getting his first lay. Juices covered her face and sprayed into her mouth with burning force. Soon, the thundering flood subsided and Jeanette's body went limp. When it was over, Amber climbed up next to her sister-in-law and kissed her gently on the mouth. The two young women held each other and kissed while Jeanette recuperated. Amber couldn't wait until it was her turn to feel what it was like to have another woman between her legs.

3 THE ANNIVERSARY GIFT

Beatrice the Saleswoman

Sheila walked into the lingerie store with the biggest smile on her face. Today was her tenth wedding anniversary and she wanted to pick out something naughty to wear for her husband that night. Sheila had the perfect figure for lingerie. Her hips were very curvaceous and her breasts were large enough to create the most delectable cleavage anyone had ever seen. Sheila skin was pretty fair, being a redhead, and she had the cutest freckles on the top of her chest and back.

Her husband, Mike, loved it when she wore a sexy, lacy outfit and usually shopped with her but he had been scheduled for overtime at work. No matter, Sheila was sure she could find something to their liking. As she perused the racks of naughty lace, the most gorgeous saleswoman headed her way. The woman was stunning, to put it lightly. Her raven hair framed the most beautiful face Sheila had ever seen but her eyes were to die for. The woman had the most exotic, piercing eyes she had ever encountered.

"Can I help you find anything?" the woman asked. Sheila nearly melted at the smooth sexiness of the woman's voice. Sheila wasn't into women but had to admit that this saleswoman was the total package. She seemed to ooze eroticism from every pore.

"I'm just looking, thanks," Sheila said with a smile. Beatrice, as the name read on the nametag, looked her up and down slowly as if she were undressing Sheila with her eyes. Sheila was a bit taken back.

"Come with me," Beatrice said then gave her a wink. "I know just the thing for you."

"Thanks," Sheila said and followed the woman towards the back of the boutique. As they walked, she couldn't help but stare at Beatrice's ass. It was amazing. It bounced lightly with each step and her tight slacks hugged every curve deliciously. They were so tight that they made the sexiest valley between her gorgeous cheeks. For a moment, Sheila wondered what it would feel like to give Beatrice's ass a big squeeze.

The women wove through the store until Beatrice found what she was looking for. Beatrice looked Sheila over again and started looking through the rack. Sheila joined her and was delighted at all of the sexy bra and panty sets. She had intended to find a nice teddy or bustier set but as she looked through the sets, she started to think twice.

"Here you go," Beatrice said as she held up several outfits. Sheila looked at them a bit sceptically. They were dark or brightly coloured and she wasn't sure how they would look against her milky complexion. Beatrice could sense the apprehension in Sheila.

"Trust me," the saleswoman reassured her. She nodded and took the outfits from Beatrice and disappeared into the changing room.

Inside Sheila spread out the outfits to get a better look at them. She still didn't think they would look right on her but she would try them on anyway. The first outfit she tried on was a deep crimson bra and panty set with matching thigh-high stockings. It looked very sexy but she wasn't convinced it was for her.

"How you doing in there hun?" Beatrice called out from the other side of the door.

"Okay," Sheila answered then cracked

the door open to peek out. "It's nice but just don't think it looks right."

Show Me Yours

"Let me see," Beatrice said and pushed the door open a little further. Sheila stepped back to allow her to come in. Beatrice joined her inside and closed the door. Beatrice looked her over a few times and nodded.

"It's a little deep," Beatrice agreed. She picked through some of the outfits and told Sheila to take off the bra. Sheila was a bit hesitant at first but told herself she was being silly and reminded herself that Beatrice probably did this all the time.

Beatrice turned Sheila around to face the mirror. Sheila looked at herself in the mirror and noticed that her nipples were hard. She hoped her newfound helper didn't take it the wrong way then she caught a glimpse of Beatrice in the mirror. She must have noticed her nipples because she gave a brief, sultry smile then picked up a few bras.

Sheila stood there very still as Beatrice reached around and wrapped the bras across her breasts. As they "tried on" the bras, every once in a while Sheila would feel Beatrice's chest brush against her back. Again, Sheila had never been into women but the incidental contact was starting to affect her. When they were done they still hadn't found one the two agreed on.

"I think I know the perfect one," Beatrice said and started to unbutton her blouse.

Sheila watched her in the mirror and some rather naughty thoughts started to creep into her mind. She closed her eyes for a moment and told herself not to jump to conclusions. Beatrice was a professional after all. Beatrice unbuttoned her blouse just below her chest and peeled the fabric away from her breasts.

"What do you think?" Beatrice asked.

"They're beautiful," Sheila stammered after turning around to see Beatrice's large breasts framed by an exquisite bra. "I mean, I love the bra."

"Yeah, it's my favourite," Beatrice told her. "We sell a line of them here too. Feel how soft it is."

Those last words nearly floored Sheila. She was caught completely off guard and her face showed it. Beatrice giggled a little.

"I'm not inviting you to feel me up, if that's what you're thinking," Beatrice reassured her, took Sheila's hand, and put it on her breast. Sheila stood there frozen and wasn't sure what to do. Beatrice smiled and moved Sheila's hand on her breast slightly to feel the silkiness of the bra.

"See?" Beatrice asked.

"It's very nice," Sheila replied politely. Just as she was about to pull her hand away, Beatrice squeezed her hand ever so slightly on her covered breast.

"Yes, I'd like to try one of those," Sheila said nearly breathlessly. She couldn't believe that Beatrice made her fondle her tit. She had to have been imagining it.

"Strip down, I'll be right back," the woman said cheerfully then slipped out of the dressing room. Sheila noticed that Beatrice hadn't re-buttoned her top. She had simply pulled her blouse back over her chest before leaving.

"What is going on?" Sheila asked herself quietly. She swore that Beatrice was trying to seduce her and admitted that the woman was doing a rather good job.

She peeled off the panties she had tried and felt the cool air wash over her moistening pussy. She reached down and touched herself and was surprised at how wet she had become. She couldn't believe she was being turned on by another woman. She rubbed her clit gently and cooed. She thought about the young woman as she rubbed herself. A few minutes later, she heard footsteps approaching and she quickly rolled off the stockings and waited.

"Here we go," Beatrice smiled. "Same

pattern but just a little different cut."

Beatrice sat the bra and stockings on the little bench in the changing room then knelt in front of Sheila. She opened the thong panties up and nodded for Sheila to step into them. Sheila did and felt a shiver run up her spine as Beatrice started to slide the panties on. She held her breath as she realized that Beatrice's face was inches from her bare, wet pussy. She was sure the saleswoman could smell it.

Beatrice smoothed out the fabric of the panties in the front. Sheila quivered at the errant touch of Beatrice's fingers on her skin just mere inches away from her aching quim. When she was done, Beatrice turned Sheila round and straightened the back of the thong. She cupped one of Sheila's round cheeks and lifted it to set the panty. Though the touch was brief, its effect lingered much longer.

Next, the woman took the stockings and rolled them up. Sheila stepped into them one at a time and Beatrice rolled them up her smooth silky legs. If she was trying to seduce Sheila into wanting her, she had succeeded long before the stockings. Sheila just held her breath and hoped it would be over soon.

Sheila nabbed the bra before Beatrice had the chance. She slipped it on and snapped the front clasp quickly. She tried to work the bra over her breast but

Beatrice gave a playful tusk.

"It's a half-cup bra, dear," Beatrice said with wry smile.

"Oh!" Sheila replied in surprise. She was expecting one like the bra the other woman was wearing.

"I thought it would look nicer, see?" Beatrice said and turned Sheila to face the mirror. "You have wonderful breasts and perky nips, so why not show them of? Besides, I'm sure your husband would love it."

Sheila had never thought of that and for the first time since Beatrice had joined her in the dressing room she thought of her husband instead the saleswoman. She stood there and marvelled at the image that stared back at her in the mirror. She was dead sexy, no doubt, and knew Mike would love the outfit.

"If I were your husband I'd definitely love that bra over mine," Beatrice said and pulled Sheila's thoughts back to her. The young woman quickly shed her bra and slacks and stood next to Sheila with a smile.

"See?" she asked Sheila. "If you were a man, which would you prefer?"

Sheila stared at them for a moment. She eyed herself then shifted her gaze to Beatrice. It was a tough decision. Beatrice's breasts were larger than hers were and so the bra she was wearing made the most enticing cleavage. But Sheila's breasts were nice too and the half-cup bra looked stunning.

"I'd probably be happy with either," Sheila admitted.

"Men like easy access, right?" Beatrice asked. Sheila had never thought of that before but Mike seemed to like it when she wore looser lingerie.

"I suppose so," Sheila answered with a nod.

"It's not a 'suppose so', it's a fact," Beatrice responded. "Say you were a man, without taking off my bra; show me how you'd expose my breasts."

"Excuse me?" Sheila blurted in surprise.

"It's okay, just show me."

Sheila shrugged and played it cool but inside she trembled. She was hot and Beatrice was just making it worse. She swore the woman was torturing her on purpose. Sheila took a deep breath and slid her fingers under the top of Beatrice's bra. She was amazed at how soft the woman's breasts were to her touch. When she brushed her fingers over Beatrice's nipples, they were hard and she thought she heard a soft moan escape the woman's lips.

Sheila struggled a bit with the bra. It wasn't tight but the straps weren't very forgiving. Coupled with the size of

Beatrice's breasts it took several tries and different approaches to finally get the bra folded down to expose her deliciously round breasts. Sheila stared at them for a moment in awe. She wanted to reach out and feel them. She wanted to take them in her hands, squeeze them, and do all kinds of naughty things with them.

"Not as easy as it seemed, was it?" Beatrice asked. Her voice had a slight tremble to it and Sheila noticed it right away. Sheila shook her head.

You Can Have Mine

Sheila shook her head and took Beatrice's hands. Both women stood there and stared at each other in silence. Sheila slowly backed Beatrice up against the wall and leaned in to kiss her. Beatrice closed her eyes and Sheila could see her lips quivering.

"What are you doing?" Beatrice asked breathlessly.

"Shhh," Sheila cooed then kissed Beatrice deeply. Both women moaned as their tongues danced together. The feeling of kissing another woman was exquisite. Beatrice had woken a sinful side in Sheila and she was intent on exploring it completely.

"Stop, please," Beatrice pleaded feebly

as Sheila started kissing and sucking along the side of her neck. Sheila started rubbing her body harder against Beatrice with every plea that slipped out between her moans. There was no stopping her. She was hot and it was the young woman's fault, and she was going to make her pay ever so blissfully.

Slowly Sheila moved further down Beatrice's body. Her lips and tongue tasted every inch of that soft succulent body. The saleswoman was breathing harder with each sizzling touch upon her body. Her hands manipulated her large tits roughly. Sheila watched Beatrice tease her nipples and slid a hand down to her own dripping pussy to rub it through her panties.

"Turn around," Sheila ordered Beatrice.

"Yes ma'am," the young woman replied submissively and did as she was told.

Sheila swooned for the woman. She couldn't believe that this woman was actually very submissive after the forwardness she displayed earlier. Sheila knew this would be fun even though it was uncharted territory for her. She took a breath and pulled Beatrice's panties down. She stared at that perfect ass and in a moment would finally see how good it felt to squeeze it.

Sheila grabbed Beatrice's round cheeks roughly in each hand and shoved her face between them. Beatrice forced her ass back on her face as Sheila lashed her tongue out clumsily. Sheila licked every which way she could. She didn't know exactly what she was doing but by Beatrice's reaction, she figured she was doing something right.

Beatrice bit her lower lip as Sheila's tongue licked roughly through her pussy. She ground her ass harder against Sheila's face as her hands travelled the wall looking for something to hold onto. Sheila was in heaven. She tasted another woman's pussy for the first time and was hooked. She screwed her tongue in and out of the young woman's juicy cunt over and over while she squeezed and spanked her soft, round ass.

Sheila spread Beatrice's ass then slid two fingers up her sopping cunt. She pumped and twisted them in and out roughly. Beatrice moaned and bucked her hips wildly. Sheila reached up and grabbed a handful of her new slave's long, raven hair and pulled.

"Do you still want me to stop?" she teased Beatrice.

"No ma'am," Beatrice gasped out. "Please no."

Sheila shoved her face back into Beatrice's ass again. She lashed her tongue out over the woman's tight asshole and felt the sudden trickle of Beatrice's cum down her arm. Beatrice moaned loudly as she came. Her ass bounced uncontrollably and helplessly against Sheila's relentless pleasuring.

When it was over, Sheila stood up and turned Beatrice around to face her. She kissed her deeply then smiled. She knew she had found the perfect anniversary gift to bring home to her husband. Beatrice didn't resist the proposition and after dressing, followed Sheila out of the store.

Sheila wore a dreamy smile on her face as she drove home with her new very submissive friend in the passenger seat. She realized that she wasn't exactly the best lover another woman could have but was a bit more at ease when she found out that Beatrice had never been with a woman before either. Sheila looked forward to future encounters and hoped she wouldn't seem so inexperienced much longer.

When they arrived at Sheila's home, her husband was nowhere to be found. As she led Beatrice upstairs, she could hear the sink running in their master bathroom. She left the young woman in the hall and went into the bedroom to find her husband. She found him in the bathroom just finishing his shave.

Happy Anniversary

"Happy anniversary," she said slyly and kissed him deeply on the mouth.

"Mmmmm," Mike moaned into her kiss. "Happy anniversary dear."

"I have a surprise for you," she said and took his hand then led him into the bedroom. She admired her husband's physique and loved the way he looked standing there in just his boxers.

"Beatrice," Sheila called out. "Come in please."

Mike looked at his wife and arched a brow in confusion and interest then turned his eyes to the door as it opened. Beatrice walked in timidly and smiled. She was completely nude and large breasts bounced erotically with each step.

"This is Beatrice," Sheila said smoothly as she pulled the young woman to her side. Mike watched as his wife leaned in and kissed Beatrice deeply. He could see their tongues sliding in and out of each other's mouths. When they were done, his wife turned back to him.

"She's our anniversary present," Sheila said coyly. Mike just stood there astounded. He would have never imagined Sheila kissing another woman, let alone bringing another woman home for them to have sex with.

Without a word, Beatrice slid to her knees and reached out to Mike. She slowly peeled down the front of his boxers and freed his semi-hard cock. Mike couldn't help but be somewhat aroused by the young woman's hot body or the way she and his wife kissed. He was surprised he wasn't completely rock hard yet. Beatrice was intent on changing that.

The young woman parted her lips and eased just the head of Mike's cock past them. She swirled her tongue slowly in circles around his spongy tip and felt his shaft immediately grow to full length in her hands. Beatrice began sucking gently with each swirl of her tongue, readying herself to take Mike's cock into her mouth.

Sheila stripped out of her clothes and pressed her body against her husband's. They kissed passionately and she shivered as Mike's hand moved up and down her back. Sheila nibbled on his smooth shoulder and ran her hands over his chiselled body. Mike wasn't just muscular, he was cut. His time in the gym and time jogging around the neighbourhood helped see to that. And Sheila loved every bit of her man's physique.

Mike groaned deeply as Beatrice took his shaft completely into her mouth. She worked his cock like a pro. Mike loved it and so did Sheila. The sight of her man's meat disappearing into another woman's hot mouth was simply one of the most erotic things she had ever seen. The sound of Beatrice sucking and slurping on Mike's cock and the moans of pleasure coming from her husband made her pussy quiver in delight. Sheila let her husband have his pleasure for a moment longer before thinking it was time to hit the bed.

Sheila reached down and delicately took Beatrice by the hair. She pulled the young woman off of her man's throbbing shaft and led her to the bed. Sheila crawled onto the soft comforter and towed Beatrice with her. Beatrice knelt on all fours near the edge and offered her deliciously round, full ass up to Mike. Mike wasted no time taking the offer.

While her husband ran the thick head of his cock up and down Beatrice's slit to lube it with the woman's flowing juices, Sheila rolled onto her back and spread her legs. Now it was Beatrice's turn to eat her pussy. She and Beatrice exchanged lustful gazes before the young woman started nibbling gently along one of Sheila's thighs.

Beatrice started at Sheila's knee and slowly worked her way toward Sheila's steamy slit. Sheila closed her eyes to enjoy the eroticism of the kisses on her milky skin. She shivered as she felt Beatrice's tongue trace slowly up and down the crease of her thigh and pelvis. It was such a hot sensation for her. Mike had never done that to her before. It was amazing.

Beatrice's delicate fingers gently spread Sheila's glistening lips.

The young woman suddenly moaned as Mike pierced her dripping slice with the head of his cock. She reflexively lifted her soft, round ass into Sheila's husband. Mike groaned at the tightness of Beatrice's pussy and pumped his shaft into her with slow, short strokes until she loosened up more. Beatrice moaned and lowered her face into Sheila's pussy.

Sheila waited breathlessly for Beatrice's tongue to touch her. She ached all over with desire for the young woman. She hoped this would be the beginning of a very close relationship with her. How often does one encounter a stranger that invokes such dark desires in a person? Maybe once in a lifetime? Once Beatrice's tongue pressed between her swollen lips, Sheila didn't care what the answers were.

Soon the three of them were moaning heavily in the throes of heated sex. Sheila and Mike locked eyes and gazed at each other in love and lust as they used this poor, albeit very willing, young woman for their pleasure. Sheila was holding the back of Beatrice's head to keep her mouth firmly planted on her hard clit. Beatrice would swirl her tongue around it then suck on it gently as if she blowing a cock.

Meanwhile, Mike was fucking Beatrice with everything he had. The sight of his wife having her scrumptious cunt eaten out by a woman made his cock harder than it had ever been before. He held onto Beatrice's hips with a vice-like grip while he rammed his hips against her tender, sweet ass harder and harder. He never imagined in his life that he would be having a threesome with his beautiful wife and one of the most stunning women he had ever laid eyes on.

And in the middle of this sexy encounter was Beatrice. If there were a place beyond heaven, she would be there right now. She loved to be used as a sex toy and the feeling of Sheila holding her face against her juicy pussy burned her up inside. It was so naughty and made her feel like some dirty slut picked up on a street corner. Though in no way was she discounting Mark's exquisite fucking.

She had never known a man with such stamina and knew she would need a break soon. His cock filled her completely with each invasive assault on her hungry quim. She bucked her ass harder against him and moaned loudly into Sheila. She couldn't hold out much longer.

Soon enough Mark started to arch his back and growl like an angry beast. His wife knew he was about to shoot his load. As much as Sheila was willing to share her man with this woman, she wasn't about to let him cum without getting her just portion. Sheila got to her knees and pulled Beatrice off of her husband's throbbing cock.

She took Mike's cock in her hand and started pumping it fast and hard. Beatrice slid up to Sheila's side just in time to receive Mike's hot seed. Sheila pumped harder and Mike's cum erupted from his pulsing cock. His moan shook the room as his milky cum shot out in multiple spurts. The thick streams plastered Sheila's and Beatrice's waiting faces.

When he was finally done, he opened his eyes and looked down at the two women. His jizz coated their mouths and cheeks with some of it dripping off and oozing down their large, round breasts. Both women embraced and started kissing, swapping his cum between their mouths. They rubbed their bodies together and smeared his seed all over their chests.

After they had cleaned up, Sheila and Beatrice slipped under the covers and curled up on either side of Mike. The three of them embraced and drifted off into a much-needed sleep. They knew this episode was long from being over and would need their rest for later.

4 WHO NEEDS THE QUARTERBACK?

The Shower Room

"That is some fine piece of man," Jennifer Brighton giggled to her teammate, Bianca.

"You said it, girlfriend," Bianca shot back.

Both cheerleaders sat on the sideline and watched their college's star quarterback directing his offense during practice. Mark Sedgewick was in his senior year and was the front-runner for the Heisman Trophy this year. At 6'5", 245 pounds, Mark's blonde haired, blue-eyed physique was the object of many of Jennifer's and the rest of the cheerleaders' fantasies.

"I'd love to get me some of that white meat," Bianca said.

"I'm sure you would," Jennifer swatted Bianca on her caramel-kissed, ebony shoulder.

Two agonizing hours later, practice was over and the cheer squad hit the locker room. By the time Jennifer finished going over some new routines with her coach and squad captain, the locker room was virtually empty. There were a couple of girls left getting dressed, but soon she'd be alone. Being alone was usually dangerous for her.

Jennifer was perpetually horny, plain and simple. She couldn't fall asleep at night without masturbating to at least two orgasms. She had a whole library of porn on her laptop and watched everything from gangbangs to lesbians. Her only preference involved men that looked like Mark. She imagined herself being the object of the Mark-like actor's sexual campaign. She even had a roommate move out because of her obsession with sex.

She quickly undressed and hit the showers. She cranked up the hot water and waited until it was nice and steaming before stepping under the soothing, penetrating streams. Jennifer closed her eyes and relaxed. As she smoothed the water over her tense body, she felt the familiar want begin to stir in her pussy.

She smiled.

Jennifer had many fond memories of these showers. She hadn't had any recently but she remembered the last one. She had walked in on two of her squadmates making out once and she rubbed herself off spying on them. Jennifer could feel her juices flowing now and tried to recall the encounter. At the first touch of her hands on her breasts, the image in her mind shifted from the two girls to Mark.

She lost herself completely in the fantasy. She cupped her soft, round, glistening tits and squeezed them gently as she imagined Mark would do. Jennifer backed herself up against the wet, tiled wall and let the shower run down over the front of her head. Her skin was soft and smooth but the water made her fondling feel so much more erotic.

Jennifer gently rubbed her young, round ass along the slick wall and cooed. She imagined Mark's hands squeezing her soft cheeks as they kissed passionately. She squeezed her breasts harder and palmed her hard, sensitive nipples. Her body trembled lightly under the tiny shocks of ecstasy that radiated through her body from her nipples. She could make herself have an orgasm just by playing with her tits.

Slowly she slid down the wall until she was crouched, sitting on her heels and her legs were spread wide in front of her. Jennifer's breathing became deeper as she entrenched herself further into her fantasy. She pictured Mark's face between her spread thighs, eating out her shaved, succulent pussy. She moaned softly as she ran her hand down her flat tummy and over her burning cunt.

Her inner folds were already flaring past her puffy outer lips and parted to welcome her fingers that rubbed through them deeply. All she could think of was Mark and the kind of stud he must be. Jennifer slipped a finger into her burning slit and arched her head forward in pleasure. It felt wonderful, just like always, but it didn't feel right, not by a long shot.

Jennifer imagined Mark's cock had to be bigger than her finger so she slipped a second one deep into her melting slit. Her soft moan echoed off the shower walls as she fucked herself. She was getting hotter by the second. The steam of the hot water made it even hotter and soon with her eyes closed she started to groan loudly.

"Fuck me Mark," she whispered to herself. "Fuck me like an all-star sex machine."

In her throes of pleasure, she added a third finger in her sopping cunt. Jennifer stretched her pussy to the breaking point and loved every moment of it. She twisted and pulled feverishly on her sore, sensitive nipples as if she were trying to rip them off. Her hips had mind of their own now and pumped forward against her hand as she palmed her clit roughly.

She could feel her orgasm mounting and knew it wouldn't before long before her pussy would constrict around Mark's beautiful cock in animalistic bliss. Harder Jennifer pumped her fingers deep into herself. She fucked herself like crazy, trying to push herself over the edge and into the abyss of pleasure. She had self-gratification down to an art form.

Jennifer's chest heaved and her heavy breasts bounced gently beneath her deep, ragged breaths. She searched the shower room wall with her free hand to find something to grab onto, to steady her at the apex of her passion. Harder, she finger-fucked herself. She ravaged her pussy as hard and fast as she could despite the resistance of her angry, tired muscles.

Her eyes rolled into up into the back of her head and she screamed as she came. Her body shook violently and her feet slipped out from beneath her. She rolled back and forth on the floor and stretched her arm out for anything to anchor her. Jennifer's legs shook and her stretched, sore pussy clenched around her fingers. All she could do was ride the wave of euphoria until she came back to earth.

Soon her orgasm subsided and she was able to collect herself again. She had needed that but then again, she always needed that. She looked around quickly and aimed to finish her shower before anyone could walk in her.

When she was done, she wrapped a towel around herself and left the shower room. Near the corner of its entrance she found a small towel lying on the floor. She looked at it and thought for a moment. She hadn't noticed it on her way in. Jennifer shrugged it off and made for her locker.

The Aftermath

The next week was pretty typical for her. She went to class, went to practice, and of course squeezed in a masturbation session or two every day. Each time she fingered herself she thought of Mark. She had to have him and made up her mind that she was going to make a play on him sometime during the weekend.

"What's his problem?" Bianca asked Jennifer and jerked her head toward Jake, the equipment manager.

"I dunno, but he's been acting weird lately," Jennifer replied as she and the rest of their squad stretched.

"You'd think he'd never seen us bending over before," the other cheerleader mentioned.

"Yeah," Jennifer grunted as she

stretched to the left. "He's been staring at me all week. And when I say hi or something he just looks away and disappears."

Bianca giggled, "I think somebody likes you!"

"Whatever," Jennifer shot back.

During the rest of the practice, Jennifer thought about Jake. She wondered what was going on. He was always cheerful and friendly but he seemed to be avoiding her. She decided she'd corner him somewhere and find out once and for all what his problem was, even if she had to beat it out of him.

Jake was a handsome young man. He wasn't the typical geeky towel boy or wannabe athlete that took care of the equipment because he couldn't make the cut. He really had a lot going for him but the question still nagged at her. When practice was over, she made a beeline for the equipment room.

"Jake," Jennifer announced herself as she slipped into the equipment room and shut the door. Jake looked startled by her sudden appearance and visibly became nervous.

"Hi," he said in an uncharacteristically flat tone.

"We got a problem and we need to get it settled now," she demanded.

"Ummm, I, what are you talking about?"

Jake responded as he fidgeted with a football helmet.

"What's the story, huh?" Jennifer walked toward him. Jake tried to keep his distance but soon found himself cornered.

"You've been looking at me all weird and stuff this week," she accused him firmly. "You haven't said two words to me and I'm getting sick of it. So spill it. What's the problem?"

Jake looked at her for a moment then his eyes looked around as if he were trying to plan an escape. Jennifer snatched the helmet from his hands and absently tossed it across the room. She stood there with her hands on her hips and wasn't about to leave until she got an answer.

"Fine," Jake said and started to rub his forehead. Jennifer eyed him as he paced back and forth a few steps nervously.

"I saw you," he admitted and leveled his gaze at her.

"What do you mean you saw me?" she demanded.

"Last week, in the shower," Jake's voice trailed off.

Jennifer looked at him oddly then shifted her eyes around the room. She shook her head slightly. So he saw her in the shower? No big deal, she was sure he liked what he saw but still wasn't sure about the whole thing.

"So?" she said. "So you saw me

showering."

Jake shook his head and looked at her evenly. "You weren't showering."

Her eyes opened wide in surprise and she suddenly remembered. That day. When she had the most sinful of fantasies about Mark. When she fucked herself until her pussy begged her to stop. That day. She remembered seeing a towel on the floor and never really thought about it until now.

Jennifer looked at him skeptically. She guessed she could live with him seeing her masturbate. It's not like she could undo that now. Her eyes strayed a little as she thought and wasn't quite sure what to say. Jennifer looked at Jake and smiled.

Reconciliation

She dropped to her knees and looked up at Jake. His eyes were wide in surprise but the front of his shorts was already bulging. Jennifer figured he was already hard thinking about watching her fuck herself that day. She didn't blame him; she would have loved to see herself fingering her sweet pussy, too. Maybe one day she'd have to record it.

Jake closed his eyes and waited as Jennifer slid down his shorts to unveil one of the most gorgeous cocks she had ever seen. It wasn't overly huge, about eight inches, but it was smooth with a perfectly proportionate glans. Jennifer dove on it immediately and shoved the spongy head into her mouth.

Jake groaned as she gobbled on his cock like she was starving. Jennifer slurped and sucked feverishly on his stiff dick. She held it halfway in her mouth and let her tongue snake slowly around the rim of his cockhead. Her fingers wrapped around his exposed shaft and started pumping on it furiously. She was known for giving excellent head.

While Jennifer displayed her oral prowess, Jake had leaned back against the counter. He held on to the edge tightly with both hands and groaned each time she took his cock into her mouth. Jennifer could feel the juices oozing from her pussy and shoved a hand down the exercise shorts under her shirt and started to finger her clit. Each time she flicked her clit with her finger, her pussy twitched and flared with deep desire.

Jennifer's head bobbed on and off of Jake's stiff dick quickly. Each time she took him all the way in, she could feel the pulsing head of his cock slide down her throat an inch or two and would swallow hard to massage it with her throat. Jake's breathing was deep and rapid and she knew she was living up to her reputation.

Jake must have agreed, because soon he had his hands on her head and was pumping his hips into her face, fucking her mouth relentlessly. Jennifer moaned on his smooth, throbbing shaft. The quickness of his thrusts into her throat forced her saliva out past her gripping lips. Her spit ran down her chin and dripped off in long, stringy tendrils. The entire chest of her uniform was soaked with her saliva.

She was loving every second. She had already slid two fingers past her flaring lips and fucked her slimy cunt. The heat rose deep inside of her and she burned to have Jake take her but was enjoying sucking him off too damn much. Jennifer's cheeks sunk in each time she sucked his cock. Her mouth was like a vacuum and she could feel every inch of his glorious dick as he pounded her face.

Suddenly Jake popped his bouncing dick from her mouth. He pulled her to her feet roughly, turned her around, and bent her over the round table in the center of the locker. Her exercise shorts and panties quickly found themselves piled up in a corner with her skirt pulled up over her soft, inviting ass. Jennifer bounced her ass enticingly at Jake, begging him to fuck her wildly.

Jake did. He shoved his raging cock into her sloppy, loose pussy and started fucking her long and hard. Jennifer grunted in pleasure each time his hips rammed into her succulent ass. She held on to the table and moved her ass to match his thrusts. Jake's cock felt wonderful each time it invaded her quivering cunt and filled her up.

Jennifer would have never imagined Jake could be like this. She wondered if she had been fantasizing about the wrong man. Who needed the quarterback when the towel boy did just fine? She didn't. Jennifer succumbed to her desire and let him have his way with her.

Each thrust brought her closer to the edge but she needed him deeper. She needed to feel his cock fill her completely up. So Jennifer reached back and grabbed her ass. She spread her cheeks wide to allow Jake to penetrate her as deeply as he could. He had one hand pressing on the small of her back as he rode her like the sultry nympho cheerleader she was.

Higher and higher, the bliss and desire rose inside of her. She had never been fucked so furiously in her life. Just when she thought it couldn't feel any better, Jake slipped his thumb past her tight ring and into her ass. She exploded.

Jennifer wailed in the midst of the terrible, angry waves of pleasure washing over her. She came and came and her orgasm continued to take her to new heights with each animalistic thrust of Jake's cock. Soon she could feel his dick throb hard and expand inside of her and knew he was about to cum.

She could feel his thrusts getting shorter and sharper as his delicious seed readied to fill her. A few seconds later, he did. His cock erupted inside of her and spewed what felt like a gallon of cum into her waiting cunt. Jake shot so much cum into her that it leaked past her gripping pussy lips and ran down the back of her thighs. The sensation of his steaming jizz boiling in her wanton quim and oozing down her legs was intensely erotic.

When they were done, Jennifer pulled her panties and shorts back on without bothering to clean herself off. She gave Jake a wink and told him to be in the equipment room every day, right after practice. After all, who needs the quarterback?

5 SEXY SPANISH

The Pupil

"Buenas tardes," Maria greeted her pupil.

"Buenas tardes," Jason replied.

Maria Contreras smiled sweetly at Jason then led him back to the private study room she had reserved in the library. She was finishing up her Master's degree this year so she only had a few classes. She used her spare time to take on extra students for Spanish tutoring; after all, she was Mexican and grew up speaking the language. Jason had been a client of hers for the past two semesters.

It confounded her as to how he

struggled to learn the language the first time around and yet signed up for another Spanish class. Maria wondered why that was. He had already satisfied his degree requirements with the first class. Maybe he genuinely wanted to learn the language, and since the tutoring was free, he figured he might as well take it.

It was funny how few students actually took advantage of the tutoring program at school. The school hired tutors based on their specialties and experience, so there was never an out-of-pocket cost to the pupils. So many of them spent good money on private tutors thinking they would get better service when a lot of the private tutors were registered with and available at no charge through the school.

Maria admitted that there had been times she got the feeling that Jason liked her. Who'd have blamed him? Maria was quite stunning. She always dressed professionally, even when attending classes. Her milky smooth skin was sun-kissed enough to appear she was wearing makeup though she rarely did. She'd line and shadow her eyes and color her lips a very soft, natural color, but aside from that, her glowing face was all-natural.

Maria glanced back at Jason to ask him something as they wove their way through the library. His eyes shifted up to meet hers, and he offered a small smile. She returned the smile sweetly. Maria's smile grew bigger after turning her attention back in front of her. Had she just caught him checking out her ass? Perhaps he was a leg man; on Maria, either one was just as beautiful as the other.

Her legs were long and shapely. They had a nice tone to them, and the hem of her skirt brushed just enough above her knees to leave any man in quiet contemplation. She had a boyfriend once that had said that her ass was her best feature. He could never keep his hands off of it. It was round and smooth, a littler larger than she would have liked, and had a soft bounce to it as she walked.

Personally, she thought her breasts were her best feature. They were large enough to create a deep, sexy crease of cleavage without the need for a special bra. Yet they were small enough not to sag much in the nude. Her nipples were about the size of a pencil eraser, perhaps slightly bigger. Her areolae were about the size of quarters and crowned her breasts perfectly.

She quashed the reverie about her body before it turned too lucid for her to manage. Maria didn't have many relationships while in college. She had too much time wrapped up in her classes and tutoring to have a boyfriend. She had only dated the last guy for a couple of months then called it quits. Despite the lack of affection and physical contact in her life, she was very sensual and sexual. Her vivid imagination and the right manipulation satisfied her quite nicely on most nights.

Self-Inspiration

Usually, it didn't take much to inspire a mind-blowing fantasy. Seeing herself in the mirror, especially naked, was overkill for inspiration; even the brief reverie she pulled herself was enough to make her rightly wet. Maria promised herself a nice candlelit interlude when she finished with Jason.

Maria unlocked the door and followed Jason inside. She paused for a moment after closing the door to give one of her ample breasts a meager squeeze. During that brief second, dozens of steamy hot images flashed through her mind.

Maria pictured herself gently massaging her legs with some warm vanilla-scented oil. She loved vanilla and could almost feel the subtle heat on her calves as it slowly worked its way up. Her eyes closed as she pictured the vivid scene in her mind. Maria stifled a moan as the fantasy blurred through her mind then slowed to a painstakingly slow pace.

Her body glowed sensually from the candlelight that kissed her oiled skin. Her arching brows and pouting lips gave her the most erotically helpless look. Her glistening breasts undulated softly with each rise and fall of her chest. Her flat stomach flexed quickly, and her hands were buried between her thighs.

As the angle changed, her knees parted and her thighs spread flatly on the flowery comforter of her bed. She was pumping her fingers of one hand furiously in and out of her freshly shaven pussy while massaging her clit with the other. Maria caught her breath for a moment and suddenly realized where she was.

Her eyes flung open in surprise and immediately found Jason staring at her. The look of shock on his face was amplified by the gaping of his mouth. Maria removed her hand from within her blouse. She had unbuttoned it just enough to slide her hand in and beneath her bra to massage her bare breast. Her nipples were visibly hard through the fabric of her shirt.

"I'm sorry," Martha stammered and excused herself.

Inside the restroom, she was leaning on the counter and breathing quickly. She felt like she was going to hyperventilate or vomit, neither of which would ease the embarrassment she'd feel returning to the study room. As she calmed down a bit and splashed some water on her face, Maria felt deeply ashamed of herself.

She cursed at the reflection in the mirror. She told herself that she'd not have her bouts of eroticism if she had simply made the time to have a meaningful relationship with someone. Hell! It didn't even need to be meaningful, as long as she got laid now and then. Maria couldn't imagine what had been going through Jason's mind.

Clearly, he was shocked and probably pegged her for some kind of nymphomaniac. Then again, he had been her pupil for nearly the past year and knew a little about her personal life, so maybe he just thought she lost control of her urges for whatever reason. Maria brought her hands up to her face and shook her head. Maybe he thought she was making a pass at him, giving him some kind of invitation to fuck her.

Perhaps she was. If Jason had taken her brief moment of weakness as a come-on and decided to act on it, would she let him? Maria thought long and hard about it. In many ways she might; she needed the physicality of it. That sounded nice and all, but she didn't want to get bogged down in a relationship so close to graduating.

Calm and Cool

Maria took a deep breath to compose herself and headed back to the study room. She saw Jason walking toward the front of the library. He had his backpack looped over his shoulder. Quickly, she shuffled over to him and touched him on the arm.

"Where are you going?" she asked.

"I thought that...," he stammered back.

"Come on," she said and nodded toward their private room. Jason nodded and followed her back.

"Jason," Maria started after closing the door behind them. "I want to say that I'm so sorry."

Jason waved his hands and shook his head. "I'm good, Maria. If you're still up to it, I'd still like the tutoring."

Maria nodded and pursed her lips into a small smile. She was grateful Jason had cut her off because she wasn't exactly sure what she was going to say to him. Maria settled in next to him at the table, and they started their session.

It was agonizing for her to sit through the tutoring. The whole time her mind was stuck on the moment, she fondled her tit in front of Jason. As she thought about it longer, the feeling of shame inside of her slowly churned into something more erotic, more needful. It consumed her and left a swelling feeling of emptiness.

Tutor Time

Maria couldn't take it anymore and looked at Jason with hungry eyes. She reasoned with herself inside and stood up. He watched her intently as if he knew what was going to happen. Maria locked the door and begun unbuttoning her shirt. In no time she was standing there in just her bra and panties.

She watched Jason's eyes drink her in and saw the bulge rising in his pants. Slowly she reached back and unclasped her white, lacy bra. Jason groaned at the sight of her magnificent breasts. Her nipples were already hard, and she teased them with the tips of her fingers.

When Jason turned in his chair to face her more completely, Maria dropped to her knees and freed his semihard cock. Jason closed his eyes and lounged back in the chair to enjoy the attention she was about to give him. Her eyes examined his shaft up and down. She could already feel it inside of her and fought the urge to mount him right away and ride him to a much-needed orgasm.

Maria's nimble fingers danced over the smoothness of his cock, willing it to life before her eyes. She lowered her mouth to its head and licked it slowly with her sinful tongue. Jason inhaled sharply at the soft, wet contact on his glans. She rubbed his cock all over her face as she worshipped its power to fulfill her needs and desires.

She moaned at the smooth hardness of

his shaft on her cheek. Jason's pre-cum drew thin, glistening lines across her face as she massaged his rod with her fingers and cheeks. She teased its head with her lips then sucked it into the warmth of her mouth. Maria moaned onto his cock as she swirled her tongue around its length and sucked gently.

Her free hand roamed her chest, alternating between squeezing her bountiful tits and teasing her hard, sensitive nipples. Her eyes were closed as she continued to orally pleasure Jason. She pictured herself in his lap, her hips rising and falling as she fucked him. This spurred the desire that was growing like a silent thunder inside her.

Maria started stroking his cock faster and harder. She worked more of his length into her mouth until she felt the tip press against the top of her throat. Jason's stifled moans drove her anticipation higher. She wanted him inside of her badly but forced herself to continue sucking his cock and enjoy the moment.

She relaxed her throat enough to allow his long dick to slide down it an inch or two. She swallowed and massaged his cockhead with her throat. Jason's shaft pulsed and throbbed in her mouth. Maria had never had much experience giving a guy a blowjob, but from the look on Jason's face and the sounds of his groans, she must be doing a good job.

Her head bobbed slowly at first then faster and more urgently. His glistening shaft disappeared time and time again into the warm depths of her wicked mouth. The heat in Maria's pussy for her student rose sharply, and she quickly had her hand stuffed inside her panties and was rubbing her clit. Her cunt was completely drenched with her juices, and she fingered herself quickly.

Maria continued to fuck Jason with her mouth. She pulled his hard dick from her mouth just long enough to take a gasping breath then sunk it inside again. She forced it completely inside to its base. She nuzzled her face in his soft pubic hair and moaned delightfully. Jason's hips had started to move gently to move his cock in and out faster and deeper.

Her tongue swirled around his shaft. She could taste every inch of his flesh and feel every tiny vein that fed his dick with hardening life. If he were to fill her mouth that very moment with his thick cum, she probably wouldn't protest. She was hot and the nastiness of the thought just made her hotter. She would have been content enough just to frig her pussy to a nice juicy climax while he pumped his load down her throat.

Suddenly, Maria popped his raging dick out of her mouth. Her panties quickly found themselves piled in a corner. She turned away from him then straddled his lap. Jason reached out, grabbed her deliciously round ass, and squeezed it. Maria guided the head of his cock to her dripping hole as she lowered herself slowly.

Once she felt his head slide through her flaring lips and into her waiting hole, she put both hands on his knees and pressed herself down. Slowly Jason watched as his cock disappeared inch by inch into her drenched slit. Her delicate lips gripped it tightly as if they were afraid to let his shaft go. Once she was completely filled, Maria just sat there and enjoyed the overwhelming euphoria. It definitely had been too long since she had a man.

Maria eased herself up and down on his raging shaft. The desire was burning her up, and she resisted the need to bounce wildly and force her orgasm prematurely. She didn't know when she would get the chance to have a man again and didn't want to waste it with superfluous fucking. Jason's hands moved over her ass and hips slowly, caressing and squeezing her body here and there.

She reveled in the tenderness of his touch. The moment was sweet and beguiling. Maria slid on and off of his shaft slowly. Her pussy was crying at the pleasure she had deprived it for so long.

Her breasts, crowned nicely with hardened nipples, bounced ever so subtly with her gentle movements. Maria's breaths were shallow and rapid as she moved her hips and ass a little faster.

Their sex continued, slow and sensually, and she could hear Jason's grunts quietly behind her. She could feel his raging cock pulse and throb inside of her burning pussy. Maria knew it wouldn't be long before Jason would be near his climax and reached down and rubbed her clit to bring her closer to hers.

Suddenly, Jason lifted her off of him. Maria was bent over and felt his cock thrust into her gaping pussy. She grunted and held on to the table as Jason started to fuck her aggressively. Her gentle, sensuous sex was replaced by the animalistic hunger that she invoked within her pupil. Maria loved it.

Harder, Jason fucked her. His cock invaded her pussy deeply and powerfully. His hips slammed into her rippling ass, reaming her dripping cunt roughly. She bit her lower lip to keep her cries of pleasure from echoing throughout the room and library. Maria reached back and spread her ass for Jason, allowing him to slide into her deeper than before.

Jason licked his thumb and forced it into her tight asshole. Maria moaned loudly and came. Her entire body was suddenly consumed with white-hot pleasure. Everything around her disappeared except for the bliss that blinded her to her surroundings. She begged Jason to fuck her with all his might. It felt like her cum poured from her clenching pussy and ran down her legs.

Jason pounded her feverishly. Her orgasm peaked and peaked again as if each massive thrust was taking her higher and higher through the throes of ecstasy. Maria's legs trembled and grew weak. The beast in Jason seemed bent on fucking her until she could no longer move. His sudden aggressiveness scared her and turned her on at the same time. It was wonderful.

Just when she thought she couldn't take it any longer, Jason pulled his cock from her aching pussy. He took her roughly by the hair and shoved her to the floor. She looked up at him just in time to catch his thick cum across her face. Jason came with the force of a dozen men. His spurting cockhead was inches from her face, and gobs of his thick jizz slapped her across the cheeks.

When he was done, he shoved his cock back into her mouth. Maria gratefully accepted it and continued to suck him dry. It was such a nasty and erotic feeling. His thick, white seed dripped from her face and glasses while she swallowed the remnants from his softening cock.

When it was all over, Jason simply stuffed his semihard dick away and thanked her for the tutoring session. He grabbed his things and stuffed her panties and bra into his backpack then left. Maria watched the door close in wonderment. She simply sat there, naked and hot and covered in Jason's cum. She stretched out on the floor and reached for her pussy.

It was soaking wet and begged for more. Since she still had the room for a couple more hours, Maria spent the time fingering herself and smearing Jason's cum all over her body. It had been a successful session, and she couldn't wait for the next one.

6 DOING THE ROOMIE

A Shocking Discovery

Evelyn was lying wide awake in bed. She had been tossing and turning all night, but her mind was working overtime. She had been told something at work that hinted at a promotion, and now she had the entire weekend to agonize over it. The only bright side was that Evelyn could sleep in, that is, if she could even fall asleep.

She rolled over onto her left side to face away from her clock in hopes that not seeing the time would help her a little. It didn't. Evelyn fought with her thoughts so she could finally fall asleep, but it was no use. She conceded that now just wasn't the time, so she decided maybe something on the television would help put her out. She wasn't banking on much being on the tube after midnight.

Evelyn stretched and got out of bed. She stepped into her white, fuzzy slippers and pulled on her robe. She typically slept in the nude and tonight was no different. Evelyn figured her roommate, Carina, would be in bed so just the robe would be fine. She grabbed a pillow and walked into the hall.

As she made her way toward the den of their house, she saw the glow of the television reflect off one of the walls. Evelyn stopped halfway through the hall. She frowned slightly because she thought Carina probably fell asleep watching T.V. and didn't want to disturb her. With that idea shot to hell, Evelyn decided that she could try reading in her room. Reading always seemed to put her to sleep.

Evelyn took a step back toward her room then stopped. She thought she heard something and figured it was the television. She waited for a few minutes to see if she heard it again. Her breaths were shallow and quiet as she strained to listen. Evelyn heard it again. It sounded like moaning. Her heart skipped a beat or two as she thought something might be wrong with her roommate. But as she continued toward the den, she realized they weren't moans of pain or sickness.

No, they were moans of pleasure.

Dozens of scenarios blazed through Evelyn's mind as she wondered just what Carina was doing. She knew she should just go back to her bedroom and read but her curiosity was piqued. Evelyn crept silently toward the end of the hallway. She held onto her pillow tightly as she braced herself for something she wasn't sure she was ready to see.

Evelyn peeked around the corner slowly and was met with the most shocking sight she had ever seen. Carina was lying on the couch, knees spread, and was masturbating. Evelyn couldn't believe her eyes. She glanced at the T.V. quickly and was shocked to see a porno on the screen. What was even more shocking is that it was a scene of two women having sex. Evelyn suddenly felt lightheaded and backed a few feet away into the corner.

To say, she was shocked would have been an understatement. Evelyn would have never guessed that Carina was into other women. Maybe not a lesbian, but definitely she was bi-sexual. It was too much for her to process, and she decided she was just going to slip into bed and try to forget what she had seen. Another soft moan echoed from the den, and Evelyn took a hesitant step toward her.

Again, she peered around the corner and looked at her roommate. Carina was lying on the couch with her head away from Evelyn. Evelyn had a completely unobstructed view of her roommate's smoothly shaven pussy. She watched as Carina's fingers danced gently over her bare slit. She would alternate rubbing her clit in tiny circles then rubbing her fingers deeply through her slit.

Her roommate was beautiful. Evelyn was in awe at the delicacy in which Carina masturbated. She seemed to be in no hurry and caressed every inch of her supple body. Carina arched her back slightly as she moved her hands slowly over her ample breasts. She rolled her hard nipples between her forefingers and thumbs, and the sexiest moan Evelyn had ever heard escaped her roommate's lips.

Evelyn had lost all track of time. She stood there, hidden in the shadow of the hall, and marveled at Carina. She watched and felt the heat begin to rise inside of her. Part of her felt ashamed for getting turned on by the woman she had just accused of being a lesbian. The other part didn't care. The other part made her slip her pillow between her thighs and grind her hardening clit against it. The other part made her picture the two of them together, kissing and touching and tasting each other like the women in the porno were doing.

Evelyn's legs began to feel like rubber

and a shock of pleasure wracked her body. She stifled a moan and couldn't believe she just came while watching her roommate fingering herself. Embarrassed and ashamed, and quite flustered, Evelyn quietly withdrew from the corner and tiptoed back to her room. Once there, she slipped into her bed and closed her eyes as tight as she could in hopes of quashing the image of Carina from her mind.

Just as Evelyn began to drift off to sleep, she heard her roommate's footsteps coming down the hall. Carina's door closed quietly. Suddenly, thoughts of her roommate came swirling to forefront of her mind again. Evelyn cursed at her bout of insomnia and rolled over. She was wide-awake again and, despite her best efforts, was unable to get the picture of Carina out of her head.

Evelyn rolled onto her back and stared at the ceiling. Her hands roamed her naked body slowly as she pictured Carina on the couch. The memory of watching her roommate sliding her fingers in and out of her dripping pussy had quite an effect on her, and she began to massage her excited clit. Evelyn closed her eyes and delved deeper into her fantasy. It was the most erotic scene she had ever imagined.

Suddenly, Evelyn's eyes flew open and she sat up abruptly. Her body trembled at the realization that she wanted Carina.

She wanted to be with her roommate. She wanted to feel Carina's lips on hers and feel their soft bodies touch as they made love to each other. Evelyn got out of bed and slipped her robe on again. She was nervous, but her desire pushed her towards her roommate's room.

Risking It All

Evelyn stood outside of Carina's bedroom and stared at the closed door. She lifted her hand hesitantly to reach for the handle then paused. She closed her eyes and took a deep breath.

"You can do this," she whispered to herself. "You want to do this."

Evelyn opened her eyes, turned the doorknob, and opened the door. She tiptoed over to Carina's bed silently. Carina was sleeping on her side with her back to Evelyn and that helped a little with her nerves. Evelyn gently lifted the covers and eased into bed beside Carina. Carina stirred a little.

"What's wrong?" Carina whispered sleepily.

"I can't sleep," Evelyn replied. Carina gave her a sympathetic groan and blindly reached back toward her. Evelyn felt Carina's hand brush over her body in several places and stifled a moan. Her roommate finally found her hand and pulled her closer to her. Evelyn inhaled sharply as she felt her body press against Carina's and felt the smoothness of her roommate's skin as she allowed her arm to be wrapped around her.

"Why not?" Carina yawned.

Her sleepy voice was sexy and husky and made Evelyn melt. When Evelyn didn't answer, Carina turned over to face her. They stared at each other for a while, one waiting for an answer, the other trying to find it. Carina's eyes were too much for Evelyn to handle and she looked down slightly, ashamed of the heat that stirred between her thighs.

The change of view didn't help matters much. She was staring at the bountiful cleavage created by her roommate's bra. She traced every line and contour she could see in the dim light of the bedroom. Evelyn wanted to bury her face in Carina's breasts right then and there.

"See something you like?" Carina whispered in a teasing manner. Evelyn hadn't realized she was staring until Carina said something. Evelyn looked back up and into her eyes.

"I saw you tonight," Evelyn said softly.

"Huh?" Carina replied. She seemed somewhat stunned.

"I couldn't sleep, so I went to watch some T.V.," Evelyn explained. "And I saw you on the couch."

"Oh god, I'm sorry," Carina said as she

buried her face in her pillow. Evelyn reached over and took Carina by the chin, gently, and turned her to face her again.

"It's okay," she told her roommate. "You don't have to be sorry. If anyone should apologize, it's me. I was the one that spied on you."

"Spied?" Evelyn's roommate asked. Evelyn nodded.

"I started to leave but something made me stay," Evelyn said.

"What?" Carina said though Evelyn was sure she knew the answer already.

"You," Evelyn admitted.

"Oh," was the only thing Carina could say.

"I was completely taken in by you," Evelyn confessed. "You were beautiful. The way you caressed yourself. The way you loved yourself. Your passion. Everything about you was simply intoxicating. And now, I can't get you out of my head."

The awkward silence finally kicked in and the two young women stared at each other. They wondered what to do next. Evelyn knew what she wanted. Carina had an idea of what Evelyn wanted, but neither woman was sure of their next step.

"Do you like women?" Evelyn asked after a while.

"I've never been with one before," Carina answered. "There was something hot about watching those two women. I know it was just a porno and fake, but it was interesting. You?"

Evelyn shrugged, "Honestly? I never thought about it until tonight. I couldn't imagine being with a man that had the kind of passion and delicacy that you had on the couch. It turned me on in a way I had never felt before."

"Really?"

"Yeah," Evelyn answered. She uncovered herself a little and peeled back her robe. Evelyn lifted her breast slightly to show Carina how hard her nipple was. "See? I'm still turned on."

Carina stared at Evelyn's breast in disbelief. Her first reaction was to reach up and touch the hard nipple, but her hand stopped just shy. Evelyn sensed the hesitation in her roommate and in herself to a degree. She wanted to feel Carina's touch on her body and leaned forward a bit to let her roommate know it was okay.

Carina's touch was electric. It sent shocks through Evelyn's body like never before. Carina touched Evelyn's hard nipple, timidly at first as if it would hurt her. But soon, Carina wasn't just touching; she caressed Evelyn's bare breast gently. When she was done, Evelyn smiled.

"Did you like it?" Evelyn asked.

"Yes," Carina admitted with a nod. "So, now what?"

"Kiss me," Evelyn whispered softly.

Acting on Desire

Carina leaned forward and brushed her lips against Evelyn's. Evelyn felt a chill run her spine at the softness of her roommate's lips. Carina brought her hand up to caress Evelyn's cheek then leaned in again. Both women kissed softly, letting their lips linger upon the others. Neither had ever kissed another woman. It was so naughty but felt so wonderful to them.

As they kissed, their hands began to explore the other's body timidly. Carina had untied Evelyn's robe and was running a delicate hand ever so gently over Evelyn's hip and thigh. Carina moaned softly against Evelyn's mouth at the feeling of her roommate's soft body. Evelyn responded by running her hand along Carina's collarbone and teased her fingertips down over the beautiful cleavage she had been so mesmerized by earlier.

Both women seemed to be in heaven. Evelyn parted her lips as Carina kissed her. Her tongue shyly licked her roommate's lips. She was burning with desire for Carina, and it took every ounce of will not to push her back and fuck her madly.

They began to kiss hungrily. Their tongues slid in and out of the other's mouth, stabbing, licking, swirling. Their bodies writhed together in a fit of urgency and desire. They wanted each other. They wanted each other more than anything in the world, even if it were for just that moment. Their hands caressed and squeezed and moved over their bodies erratically as if they couldn't touch enough.

Suddenly, Evelyn rolled Carina onto her back and slid on top of her. She spread Carina's legs and ground her hips against Carina's as she began kissing suckling her friend's neck. Carina turned her head and moaned. She couldn't believe what Evelyn was doing to her but she liked it. No, she loved it. Carina spread her legs further and lifted her hips in rhythm to Evelyn. Her pussy was on fire now, and the pressure Evelyn was putting against her clit made her bite her lower lip.

Evelyn reached under and unclasped Carina's bra. She cast it aside and dove on her roommate's breasts like an animal. She shoved her face between those deliciously large tits and started moaning. The feeling of Carina's soft breasts on her cheeks drove her insane, and she bucked her hips harder. She was in heaven and by the sound of it, so was Carina.

Carina's hands moved under Evelyn's robe and down her back. She couldn't believe how soft her roommate's skin felt. She had never felt anything smoother until she got to Evelyn's ass. Her round, succulent cheeks begged to be squeezed and massaged, and Carina wasted no time in doing just that. She grabbed them roughly and dug her fingers into their giving flesh.

Evelyn moaned and pumped her hips harder against Carina. Carina arched her back and cried out in a multitude of explicit urgings. Carina could feel the sheen of her juices smeared all over them as her friend humped her pussy furiously. She pulled on Evelyn's ass harder, urging her on, urging her not to stop, urging her to manifest the orgasm she felt building deep inside of her.

"Harder baby, fuck me harder!" Carina moaned loudly as she ground her pussy harder up against Evelyn.

Evelyn bucked her hips as hard and as fast as she could. Her mind whirred with images of lust for her roommate as she fucked her. She could feel her strength slowly giving out and tried fervently to make Carina cum. Carina's hands moved from Evelyn's ass, and she grabbed onto the bed sheets to hold on for dear life. She could feel the intense pleasure of her orgasm building toward release.

"Oh god! Oh god!" Carina moaned over and over as she thrashed her head from side to side. As she started to cum, she wrapped her legs around Evelyn's hips and forced her pussy against her as hard as she could. She groaned huskily as the waves of pleasure washed over her intensely for what seemed forever before finally collapsing.

Carina's legs fell limply to the bed, and she wrapped her arms lazily around her roommate. She stared at Evelyn's smiling face. Their eyes mirrored the intense love and lust that seemed to overwhelm them. Evelyn kissed Carina gently on the lips.

"How was it?" Evelyn asked.

"It was amazing," Carina replied through gasping breaths. Both women lay together for a while so Carina could recover. It seemed forever before Carina felt the strength return to her legs and the aftereffects of her orgasm subsided.

"God, that was so hot," Carina whispered before she shifted herself and rolled over on top of Evelyn.

"I'm glad you enjoyed it," Evelyn whispered back with a smile. Her body tingled all over in the aftermath of making Carina cum. It was such an erotic experience for her. She couldn't wait to explore her roommate's body further. She couldn't wait to suck each of Carina's hard, delicate nipples into her mouth and feed on them. She couldn't wait to taste Carina's sweet pussy and feel its heat on her mouth. She couldn't wait to do a lot of things.

An Explosive Surprise

But at the moment, Carina had other ideas. She turned Evelyn's head to the side and started kissing and sucking on her earlobes. Evelyn responded quickly by inhaling sharply and cooing. She loved the attention given to her earlobes. Given the time, she was sure she could cum just from the feeling.

Carina sucked on Evelyn's earlobe for a moment longer before making her way down along her friend's neck and chest. Carina traced her tongue slowly around one of Evelyn's taut nipples. Evelyn moaned at the sensation. She'd had guys tease her nipples before, but this was different. Carina's tongue seemed softer, gentler, and moved less urgently.

Carina peeled the other half of Evelyn's robe aside, and took her other breast in her hand. It felt so soft, so wonderful and she began to massage it gently. Evelyn arched her back at Carina's every touch. As Carina slipped Evelyn's hard, sensitive nipple into her mouth, she felt Evelyn's fingers tangle themselves in her hair. She sucked gently at first. Her tongue flicked at her roommate's nipple as she began to suck harder and feed upon Evelyn's silky flesh.

Evelyn moaned loudly. Her head spun at the pleasure Carina conjured with her lips and tongue. It was so different and so amazing. Carina took her other nipple between her fingers and rolled it back and forth, pinching and tugging gently. Carina could tell she was performing well by the way Evelyn tightened the grip on her hair.

After a few minutes, Carina started to kiss her way down Evelyn's flat stomach. She traced her tongue around Evelyn's navel and placed a gentle kiss on it before moving further. Evelyn groaned in anticipation and spread her legs wide, offering her bare, dripping pussy to Carina.

Carina slid between Evelyn's thighs. Her face was inches from her roommate's musky slit. She gazed at it for a moment. It was beautiful. It was glistening with the sheen of their mixed juices in the low light. Her first touch made Evelyn's body tremble. Evelyn was on fire and wanted Carina to feast upon her.

Carina gently spread Evelyn's puffing outer lips wide and teased the tip of her tongue ever so slowly up and down Evelyn's juicy slit. The taste of her friend's pussy made her moan. It wasn't much unlike the taste of her. When she masturbated, Carina frequently would suck on her juice-covered fingers.

Carina's licking became harder and deeper. She swirled her tongue around the entrance of Evelyn's burning cunt, feeling her friend's hips slowly start to gyrate against her. She dipped her tongue in slightly and wriggled it around. Evelyn moaned and pulled her head harder against her. Each deep breath that Carina took was full of sex and cum and drove her wilder by the minute.

Soon Carina's tongue was stabbing quickly and deeply in and out of Evelyn's pussy. Evelyn's hips rode her face in the urgency of a virgin. After all, they were both virgins, so to speak, when it came to being with another woman. Carina worked her tongue faster in and out then licked the length of her friend's slit toward her clit.

When she reached Evelyn's hard, sensitive clit, she flicked it several times with her tongue. Evelyn's body trembled in delight at the sensation of Carina's tongue swirling around her clit. But when Carina started sucking on her clit, she lost complete control.

"Mmmmmm," Evelyn moaned. "Suck my clit baby! Right there! Eat my dirty little cunt!"

Evelyn's words made Carina moan into her pussy. She couldn't imagine such language coming from her friend, and it turned her on even more so than she already was. Carina started sucking harder and started stroking Evelyn's slit with her fingers. Evelyn thrashed on the bed wildly. Her hips had a mind of their own and Carina fought hard to keep pleasuring her.

Suddenly, Carina slid two fingers deep into Evelyn dripping slice. Evelyn wailed and came like a geyser. Her juices exploded on Carina's face like a fountain. Her entire body convulsed with each massive ejaculation. Carina was caught off guard and coughed a little from the sudden stream of Evelyn's sweet nectar that sprayed into her mouth.

In one final blissful shock of ecstasy, Evelyn arched completely off the bed and growled like a ravenous beast. She collapsed, completely spent. Her body still jolted lightly and the look in her eyes seemed distant. Carina sat up and stared at her in amazement. She had never seen anyone cum as intensely as Evelyn had. She heard that women could squirt if they were turned on enough, but she had never witnessed it until now. It was amazing.

Carina crawled up the bed and nestled in next to Evelyn. They were both drenched in Evelyn's sweet, slick juices. They kissed gently and Evelyn promised to return the favor after a short nap.

7 A SWEET SURPRISE

Locked Out

Forty-two-year old Linda Branstrom came home to a locked house. She was tired and figured maybe she wasn't working the key right. After several more attempts, she gave up and knocked on the door. She hoped her husband was home; when he didn't answer the door, she found herself locked out. Today was her husband's day off, and she wondered where he was. Linda was home early so she hoped he'd be along any time.

While she waited, she walked around the front of the house to try to look into the windows, but all of the blinds were closed. Tired of waiting, she decided to venture around back to see if maybe he was out there. When she went through the gate, her eyes scanned the small backyard, but her husband, Parker, was nowhere to be found.

Frustrated and a bit miffed, Linda decided to walk back out front to wait. As she walked, she noticed something hanging from one of the handles of their French doors. It looked like an envelope, so she went to investigate. The envelope was tied to the handle with a little bow on it. Linda arched a brow in interest and plucked the note from the door.

For good measure, Linda tried the handle but it was locked, too. She sighed and unfolded the envelope. She withdrew the card and opened it. There was a key taped to the inside of it. As she read the note, she started to smile:

My Dearest Linda,

Here is the key to our home and to my heart. Inside you will find some little hints for you. Enjoy until I return.

Love,

Parker

Linda smiled at the note and used the key to unlock the door. When she went inside, the house was dim, and on the dining room table, there was a vase with a dozen roses in it. There were petals scattered all over the table. She noticed a little trail of petals leading away from the table and down the hall. With her interest piqued, Linda followed the first of her husband's little hints.

As she turned down the hall, there was an enormous sign with a big red arrow pointing to the bathroom. Linda stifled a laugh and shook her head. Parker was about as subtle as a wrecking ball. She turned the knob and opened the bathroom door. She stepped in and had her breath taken away.

The bathroom was lit by a dozen candles placed all over the room. The scent of vanilla tickled at her nose and she took a deep breath. Linda loved the smell of vanilla. The large bathtub steamed with hot water. Dozens of rose petals floated on the surface and there was an assortment of perfumed body washes and lotions lining the edge of tub.

Linda touched her hand to her chest and felt her heart pounding with love for the man that she married nearly twenty years ago. As she marveled at the scene before her, she noticed another vase of roses with another envelope on the vanity. Linda set her keys and purse down beside the roses and opened the card:

Darling,
Relax and unwind. I'll be home soon.
Love,
Parker

Linda eagerly stripped down and eased into the hot, enveloping water in the tub. She felt the stress of the day starts to melt away. She closed her eyes and enjoyed the heavenly feeling of the water caressing her body. While she soaked silently, Linda began wondering what her husband had planned. The anticipation began to creep through her body as her thoughts became more and more erotic.

While she relaxed and mulled over the sinful images in her head, she began to squeeze her thighs together. The silkiness of her skin felt very sensual as she rubbed her legs back and forth. She could feel a stirring in her loins. Linda couldn't wait for Parker to get home.

Wanting Him

Linda began to absently caress her cheek and neck with her hand. She petted and stroked herself lovingly and imagined her husband's warm breath on her neck. She gasped softly at the sensation. Her hand trailed from her neck down the top of her chest and grazed between her soft, large breasts. Linda traced the back of her fingers along the contour of her tits before gently cupping one fully with her hand.

The feeling of her hard nipple running along her palm as she caressed her breast sent tiny shocks of pleasure throughout her body. She imagined her husband touching her. She felt him tease her taut nipple with his fingers and it made her arch her back slightly. Linda moaned

Parker's name softly and began squeezing both of her breasts together. She longed for him deeply.

Linda lifted one of her legs out of the water and slid it along the edge of the tub. Her toes curled as she slowly drew a hand away from her rising chest and ran it over her smooth stomach. Further and further, she moved her hand until she grazed the inside of her thigh with her nails. She pursed her lips and exhaled slowly as her fantasy began to get hotter and fill her body with desire.

Linda's tongue moistened her lips, and she imagined her husband kissing her passionately. She could feel his strong arms holding her as they kissed and she moaned into his mouth. As their kisses deepened, the lust began to build more intensely inside of her. Linda was scarcely aware that her fingers had left her thigh and were gently massaging her hard clit.

Linda sucked two fingers into her mouth and licked them seductively. She imagined her fingers were her husband's tongue as they kissed deeper and more passionately. As they kissed, Linda could feel her heart pounding harder in her chest as the heat in her needy pussy began to build and threatened to envelop her in total bliss.

Her fingers rubbed along the sides of her clit then slid through her slippery pussy lips. She could feel how extremely wet she was, even in the steaming water. Her large breasts swayed gently in the water as her chest rose and fell with each deep, ragged breath. She was hot and horny and had her husband to thank for it.

As she slid two fingers deep inside of herself, she realized she was alone in the tub. Her powerful fantasy had taken ahold of her flesh and refused to let go. She looked down to see her other knee bent and sticking from the surface of the water. The rose petals swirled on the wake from the motion of her hand as she slid her fingers deeply in and out of her burning slit. Linda felt her orgasm beginning to build and fucked herself more urgently.

Closer and closer, she drew to her climax. The muscles in Linda's arm began to tighten from fatigue, and she knew she had to cum soon or she'd be left hanging. Linda reached down with her other hand and rubbed her clit furiously in tiny circles. The water sloshed in the tub as she moved her hips in circles. Harder and faster she fingered herself; the whole time she was thinking of her husband.

Finally, the pressure of her orgasm mounted and reached its apex. She cried out in desire as the pleasure washed through her body. She strained to keep fucking herself through her tightening pussy. Her melting quim throbbed in ecstasy until the waves of pleasure subsided and left her limp and gasping for air.

Linda smiled and slid a little further in the tub. She closed her eyes to continue her soak and wait for her husband to get home. As she thought again about what Parker had planned, Linda drifted off to a light sleep. Whatever it was, she was sure it would be marvelous.

Servitude

Linda suddenly woke up to the brush of her husband's lips against hers. It took her a moment to realize he was really there. They exchanged smiles and Parker sat down on a small stool behind the bathtub. As they talked about their day, he massaged Linda's shoulders tenderly.

"The roses are lovely," Linda cooed. Parker's hands were strong but forgiving and felt wonderful on her shoulders.

After a while, Parker stopped massaging her and stood up from his stool. He offered his hand to Linda and she accepted it with a sweet, shy smile. After Linda stepped out of the tub, Parker grabbed a towel from the vanity and turned around to look at her. She was the most amazing creature he had ever laid eyes on before.

"What?" Linda asked softly.

Parker simply shook his head and

admired her. Her body glistened from the water and rose petals errantly stuck to her soft, wet skin. Tiny drops of water slowly rolled down her body. Linda just stood there and let her husband drink in the sight. Parker leaned in and kissed her gently on the lips then smiled.

Linda's husband started to dry her off slowly. The caress of the towel across her back made Linda shiver. Her heart raced and she fought back a tear at the love and attention Parker was giving her. Slowly, he worked down her body. When Linda felt his hands brush over her ass, she pushed back against him gently, letting him know what she wanted. Parker leaned forward and placed a kiss on one of her cheeks then gave her a playful bite; she was going to get what she wanted.

When Parker was done drying Linda off, he scooped her up and carried her to the bedroom. Linda wrapped her arms around his neck and laid her head on his shoulder. She sighed contently for the man who stole her heart all those years ago.

Parker Branstrom carried his wife over the threshold and into their bedroom. Again, dozens of candles illuminated the room with a soft, serene glow. He gently laid her on the bed and turned away. Linda's gaze never left her husband as she watched him reach into the closet and pull out a box. He placed the box on the bed and opened it.

Her husband pulled out a black stocking and rolled it up. Linda sat up and offered him her foot. He delicately slid the stocking past her heel and rolled it up her leg. She stifled a moan at his touch. Linda couldn't believe he was dressing her. It was the most erotic thing she had ever felt. Finally, with both thigh-high stockings on and smoothed out and black high-heel shoes on her feet, Parker offered his hand to Linda again and pulled her to her feet.

Parker retrieved a pair of black lace, high-cut panties from the box and knelt in front of Linda. He offered them and she happily stepped into the panties. Her husband slowly slid them up her smooth, shapely legs and stopped just shy of her waist. He could smell the musk of her pussy and knew she was dripping wet.

After placing a small kiss on either side of her pelvis, Parker slipped the panties on her the rest of the way. He grabbed her hips and turned Linda around. His gentle fingers slipped under the edges of the panties and drew a line to the contour of her ass, making sure the hem of her panties was smooth. Parker gave her a kiss on the back of her thigh then dug into the box again.

Linda's lips parted into a huge smile

when she saw the lace bra in his hands. It was very sheer like the panties and was sure to give him a good view of her hard nipples, even through the fabric. Parker slid the bra on her gently. He cupped each of her large breasts and lifted them slightly to ensure a good fit. Finally, he dug into the box for something else.

His last piece was a black satin choker with a gold star, about the size of a nickel, hanging from it. He wrapped it around her throat and clasped it. When Parker was done, he gave Linda a kiss on the top of her shoulder. She cooed.

If ever she could cum from the mere thought of her husband, now was the time. Linda's pussy ached for him, and she resisted the urge to pull at her erect nipples through the lace of the bra. Parker took her by the hand and led her to the full-length mirror on the back of the door. She gazed at herself in the mirror and was lost for words. She wasn't just beautiful. Linda was absolutely stunning!

Sampling Dessert

"Oh my!" Linda said breathlessly. She didn't really know what to say.

Her husband gave her a kiss on the lips then smiled. He reached into the dresser drawer and took out their digital camera. Linda arched a brow then smiled deviously. She knew what he wanted and she was more than willing to give it to him.

Linda crawled onto the bed and struck some very naughty poses for him. He nearly broke the camera button he was mashing the button so fast and hard. She felt sexy and alive. Her favorite pose was lying on her back with her head hanging over the edge of the bed as she grabbed her tits. She was pretty hot to begin with, but now she was downright fucking horny. She needed his cock now.

She watched her husband unzip his trousers; he must have sensed what she wanted by now. Linda opened her mouth and waited to receive him. Parker pulled out his raging hard cock and teased her mouth with it. Linda wasn't in the mood to be teased too much. She grabbed his thick shaft and pulled his dick into her mouth. He groaned as she took it in to his balls.

Parker leaned forward and peeled her bra down over her breasts, freeing Linda's large, soft breasts. He loved the way they flatted into massive pillows in their completely natural glory. Linda sucked on his cock hungrily, while her husband slowly fucked her mouth. She hadn't always been able to take his dick all the way in, but lying on the bed let her naturally open her throat up to him.

Linda reached down and started rubbing her aching pussy through her soaked panties. She grunted with each thrust her husband made into her mouth. She tightened her lips, flattened her tongue, and sucked lovingly on his shaft. With each thrust in, she swallowed and squeezed her throat around Parker's throbbing cockhead. He groaned deliriously. Obviously, he had no idea just how good Linda could be with her mouth.

She writhed on the bed as she fucked her pussy with one hand and her husband fucked her mouth with his cock. Her large breasts bounced beneath Parker's hands while he pulled and jiggled her hard nipples. Linda was fully engulfed in desire and as much as she loved hearing her husband groaning from his cock in her mouth, she needed him in her.

Linda popped her husband's cock from her mouth and quickly bent over the edge of the bed and offered her ass to him. Parker wasted no time. He pulled her used panties off and stuffed his throbbing dick deep into her waiting cunt. Parker started to ride Linda hard and fast. Her large, round ass rippled as his hips slammed into her over and over.

Linda arched her back and rammed her hips back into her husband. She loved being fucked from behind, whether Parker chose to pound her pussy or stretch her tight ass, something felt so dirty about it. Linda moaned her husband's name over and over as he fucked her relentlessly.

Parker reached up and grabbed a handful of her long, silky hair and pulled. That was the part that felt so dirty about being screwed doggy-style. It made her feel like a helpless beast and Parker was her master and controlled her completely by pulling her hair. Her husband started bucking his hips harder; she knew he was about to cum.

Quickly, Linda pushed him away and knelt in front of him. She took the head of his cock in her mouth and sucked on it like a lollipop. Her slender fingers wrapped around his engorged shaft and pumped furiously. She wanted to feel his thick, salty seed all over her face. She squeezed her fingers tightly and continued to stroke him off. Her eyes stayed fixed on his grimacing face. Parker's brows were furrowed in deep concentration.

Her husband's glands throbbed in her mouth as she hungrily licked and sucked it. Linda felt his hands on hers and together they drove him over the edge. She pulled her mouth from his dick and opened wide, waiting for his jizz.

Parker exploded on her face. His thick cum spewed from the head of his cock in massive streams. His first load shot perfectly into her mouth. Linda closed her mouth while they continued to milk his cock of every drip of his seed. She closed her eyes and could feel his lovely cock painting her face with beautiful lines of his cum. She loved it.

When they were done, Linda wiped all of her husband's messy cum off her face and tits, where it had dripped, and then slid her panties back on. The feeling of Parker's jizz on her skin made her lust for him even more. He had promised a gourmet meal and she was famished, though she knew what he would have for dessert afterward.

8 SEXY MASSAGE

A Gift of Relief

Rosalinda Durant was a successful project manager for a large manufacturing company. She was in her mid-30s and had accomplished quite a bit at a young age. Her husband, Richard, was especially proud of her, but worried that the stress of her job was taking its toll on her. Lately Rosalinda, or Rosie as her husband called her, had been coming home very stressed and extremely tired.

"I'm home," Rosie announced to her husband as she closed the door and hung her purse and coat on the hall tree.

"I was beginning to wonder," Richard said with a slight frown. He had been watching the clock since about six.

"I know, but this project is a bear," she sighed and flopped down next to him on the couch. They snuggled for a while until Rosie fell asleep in Richard's arms.

The next morning Rosie yawned and stretched. She sat up and was surprised she was still on the couch. She eyed the clock and couldn't believe it was almost noon. Thankfully, it was Saturday; she didn't have to be back in the office until Monday.

Rosie's muscles were stiff and ached a bit and she groaned her way to her bedroom to take a shower. She didn't see her husband anywhere and figured he was either outside working in their yard or at the store buying stuff for their yard. Richard loved being outdoors; it was one of the reasons he loved working for their city's Public Works Department.

Rosie turned on the shower and got undressed. She put her long hair up into a bun and stared at herself in the mirror. She could definitely see the stress on her face. It made her look considerably older than she was. Then there was the rest of her body.

She got enough of a workout on her job and she ate healthy so her figure was rather trim. Her hips were wide and sloped sexily into a firm set of creamy thighs. Richard always said her best attribute was her hips and bouncy ass. She could tell; most of the time when they had sex, he would do her doggy style. Richard had his preference and she had hers.

She thought her breasts were her best feature. They weren't overly large, 34D's, but were very round with the perkiest setup nipples crowning them. She noticed her nipples were hard from the air conditioner blowing down on her. They tingled a little and she resisted the urge to touch them. She knew that if she aroused herself, she would be too tired to finish herself off or make a play to get Richard into bed.

The shower had been refreshing and Rosie felt reenergized as she dried off. When she went into the bedroom to dress, she found a little envelope waiting on the bed with a red bow on it. She smiled to herself. Richard was the sweetest man in the world. He always would do little things to pick her up at just the right time. Rosie opened the envelope and found a gift certificate for a massage at a very plush day spa. Yes, Richard was a sweet man.

Testing the Waters

Two weeks later, Rosie finally decided to use her gift certificate. The stress of her latest project was killing her, and she just couldn't find any other way to relax. She donned her sweat pants and tank top and headed off to the spa.

When she pulled up to Mrs. Luy's, she couldn't believe it was a day spa. It looked like an enormous elite resort. The architecture was somewhat in a southwest style and the landscaping was magnificent. She was sure her husband spent plenty of time poking around the flora.

Inside it was just as majestic. There were dozens of employees shuffling around quickly, attending to at least twice their number in customers. The woman at the front counter greeted her politely. She was an older Asian woman, or so Rosie surmised from the silver in the woman's hair, but her face was smooth and youthful. Rosie felt a little overwhelmed and somewhat intimidated by the experience.

The woman at the desk tapped a bell and the cutest Asian woman appeared seemingly from nowhere. She took Rosie back to a private room for the massage. Rosie stripped down and nearly jumped on the massage table. She was excited and couldn't wait to see what kind of magic the young woman could work.

During the massage, Rosie learned that the young woman's name was Mika and she was twenty-three, was single with a cat, and had been a masseuse for four years. She also learned that Mika only took private clients and was considered the premier masseuse in the metropolitan area. Over the course of the next two hours, Rosie learned just how good Mika was.

"So how was it?" Richard asked when Rosie got home.

"I feel 200% better!" she replied and kissed her husband.

She told him all of the things Mika did to her, from acupuncture to heat rocks to deep massaging. Mika had even walked on her back. Rosie could tell that Richard was getting a little aroused at her story by the growing bulge in the front of his shorts. She figured he was fantasizing about her and Mika doing it on the massage table.

Richard may have been the sweetest man she had ever known, but Rosie knew he had a very perverted mind, too. She let the moment pass and they continued on with their day. Later that night, they had some of the best sex Rosie could remember. She definitely would be going back to Mrs. Luy's.

Over the course of the next few months, Rosie turned into a regular at Mrs. Luy's. She always made her appointment with Mika and was never disappointed. In fact, she and Mika had become friends and would occasionally have lunch together; once Rosie even invited her over for dinner.

Richard couldn't take his eyes off of Mika, and Rosie knew what kinds of sinful thoughts were churning in his naughty mind. Rosie admitted to Richard that she thought Mika was pretty and actually rather sexy, but reassured him that his little fantasy would always be just that: a fantasy. The look of disappointment on her husband's face was priceless; she loved it.

A few weeks after their dinner night, Rosie was at Mrs. Luy's again after a rather stressful week. The older woman greeted her at the desk and rang the little bell. Mika showed up and took her back to the private massage room.

Feeling the Eye

"So how are you today?" Mika asked as she was getting her supplies ready.

"I'm here," Rosie answered, "so that should give you a pretty good idea."

"Don't you worry. I'll fix you up fine," Mika promised.

Rosie knew Mika would, too; she always did. While she was getting undressed, Rosie swore she saw Mika checking her out in the mirror that hung over her supply desk. She didn't know how to take the look. Normally Mika would glance back to see if she was ready, but this was different and a little disturbing.

Rosie watched her eyes glance up and down her body as she undressed, and Mika seemed to pause and stare at her ass when she bent over slightly to take off her sweat pants and panties. The heat in her cheeks was rivaled only by the heat in Mika's gaze. Rosie dismissed it as being a bit paranoid from Richard's fantasy.

When she was done undressing, Rosie stretched out on the massage table, face down, with her arms at her sides. Mika draped a towel across her large ass and wheeled her little cart over. Rosie closed her eyes and waited for her friend to work her magic.

Mika started off with some lavender oil and started rubbing it over the top of Rosie's back. Usually she started with some acupuncture, but for whatever reason, she veered from her usual routine. Mika hummed softly as she worked her fingertips into Rosie's tight muscles. Rosie groaned at the pain but could feel her tension starting to melt away.

The thing that always amazed Rosie about Mika was how soft her touch was. Mika could be pressing the tips of her fingers as hard as she could into Rosie's muscles, but it always felt smooth, like fine silk; perhaps that was why she enjoyed the massages so much.

Mika's oily hands moved over her back deftly and slowly worked down. She felt fingers, fists, and knuckles kneading into her back, slowly erasing the tension in her tight muscles. After Mika finished with her back and legs, she wiped her hands off and picked up a jar with clear, gooey gel in it.

"Want to be my guinea pig, Rosie?" Mika asked while wiggling the bottle in front of her face.

"What is it?" Rosie asked.

"It's a new technique I learned," Mika explained. "The reviews are marvelous."

Rosie nodded and closed her eyes again. She felt the cool gel touch her skin. She shuddered slightly and sighed. Mika dribbled it up and down her spine and around her back. It felt good even without Mika's touch.

"So what is this technique?" Rosie asked, then felt Mika remove the towel covering her ass.

"Instead of pressure to relieve the tension," Mika explained, "this uses fast, short, light massages to invigorate the nerves, which in turn helps relax the muscles on the surface. It works best following a more aggressive massage like the one you just got."

"Sounds interesting," Rosie murmured.

Testing the Technique

As Rosie waited for Mika to start rubbing her, she felt the gel dribble over her skin. It caught her by surprise considering Mika was dribbling it on her ass but, more specifically, in the deep valley between her cheeks. It was naughty and erotic and she could feel the gel slowly running between her cheeks and over her tight asshole. When the cool gel began creeping down her bare pussy, she stifled a moan.

This was definitely not what she expected, but it felt good and she was content to let Mika work her technique on her. She felt the masseuse's hands on her back. They rubbed over her skin quickly and in a single direction until her entire backside and legs were glistening with the thick, slimy gel.

Rosie enjoyed it immensely, especially when Mika rubbed her hands along her thighs and hips. She was getting a little turned on and felt the heat begin to stir in her pussy. Mika's fingers danced over her lower back and ass like an artist. Once she felt her friend's fingers slide between her ass cheeks, she exhaled softly and fought the urge to lift her ass in response. She began to wonder if Mika was trying to seduce her.

When she felt Mika's hands leave her body, she gave a sigh of relief. She admitted to herself that her body was on fire and if Richard were here, she would have fucked him like a mad woman. While

Mika fumbled with her supplies, Rosie squeezed her thighs together and pressed her hips against the table. The pressure sent tiny waves of pleasure washing through her body and she could smell the musky aroma from her pussy begin to fill the room.

Rosie was too preoccupied with her subtle self-manipulation to notice Mika. Mika had stripped completely naked and covered her body with some of the gel. She poured an ample amount of the gel over Rosie's back. The sudden touch of the gel surprised Rosie and she quickly relaxed her body. All she had done was make her desire even worse.

Rosie felt the smoothness of Mika's thighs on her as the masseuse climbed on the table and straddled her round, succulent ass. She moaned and reflexively lifted her ass up into Mika's pussy. Rosie felt Mika's body slowly press down on her. When the masseuse's breasts touched her skin, a moan escaped her lips.

"Mmmmm," Rosie moaned softly.

Mika moved her body up and down over Rosie's. Rosie felt Mika's hands on her shoulders and neck, using her body for leverage against the slick glide of the gel. The pressure of Mika's hips against her ass was breathtaking. Rosie gently rolled her ass and felt Mika respond. Mika started humping her hips against Rosie's ass. The lithe Asian woman bent her neck and started kissing Rosie on the back of her neck.

Rosie could hardly contain herself. She burned with desire for her friend now and was resisting the urge to roll over and let Mika fuck her every which way she could imagine. Mika's hips slapped against her ass harder and Rosie pumped her hips in rhythm. She wanted her so badly right now.

Finally she couldn't resist any longer. Rosie rolled over onto her back and pulled the beautiful Asian down on her. Rosie spread her legs and wrapped them around Mika's as she began to kiss her. Their lips met passionately and their tongues hungrily slid into the other's mouth. They kissed hungrily and sucked on each other's tongue.

Rosie moved her hands along Mika's back and grabbed her ass roughly. She pulled Mika's hips into her and ground her pussy against them. Both women moaned as their bodies writhed together in sinful pleasure. Their bodies glistened from the gel smeared from Mika's body. Their shiny breasts rubbed and smashed together and when their nipples touched, Rosie felt her pussy explode in a tiny orgasm.

Mika's hips moved faster, rubbing and grinding against Rosie's dripping, hungry pussy. The room was full of the sounds of their fervent screwing. Suddenly Mika slid down Rosie's body. Rosie arched her back in sweet anticipation and wasn't disappointed. She felt Mika's sticky, slick fingers slide easily into her hot, burning cunt.

Rosie cried out in pleasure and bucked her hips wildly. Mika pumped her fingers into Rosie's glistening pussy as fast as she could. Rosie grabbed Mika's hair and shoved her face against her burning slit. Mika's wet, soft tongue licked circles around her clit, driving her insane from the pleasure. If only Richard could see them now, Rosie thought.

Mika lapped and sucked Rosie's clit viciously. Each lash of her tongue sent spasms throughout Rosie's body. Rosie massaged her shiny tits and fingered her hard, sensitive nipples. She squeezed them between her fingers and rolled them gently. The slurping sound of Mika finger fucking her drove her insane. It sounded so sinful and made her feel dirty and raunchy.

Rosie continued to pleasure her nipples. She was stroking the tiny length of them, up and down, as if she were stroking her husband's cock. She imagined it was Mika sucking on them and the thought spiraled through her in white-hot desire. Rosie was dizzy with euphoria and couldn't imagine feeling any more pleasure than she was at that very moment. She was wrong.

Mika pulled her juicy fingers from Rosie's gaping pussy. She rubbed them around her tight ass pucker and Rosie groaned loudly. She started to scream a high-pitched wail when she felt Mika's fingers invade her tight ass.

"Oh fuck!" Rosie shouted and moved her hips up and down. "Fuck my ass! Oh God! Treat me like a whore!"

Mika obeyed and soon had her fingers twisting and thrusting deep into Rosie's tight asshole. Rosie grabbed onto the edge of the massage table and held on for dear life. Her ass bounced off of the table and the gel made squishing noises each time.

Mika dove back down onto Rosie's pussy and stabbed her tongue deep into her client's melting hole. She ate her as if she were starving. Her tongue explored every crevice as she continued to fuck her ass. Rosie's head thrashed side to side in blinding pleasure. She could feel her orgasm starting to build. Rosie was in heaven and shouted every trashy urging she could to her friend.

"I'm going to cummmmm!" Rosie moaned loudly. "Yes baby! I'm almost there! Uh uh uh!"

Mika shoved two fingers from her other hand deep into Rosie's pussy and double-fucked her furiously. Rosie kicked her legs wildly as if trying to escape the brutal assault on her holes. Suddenly she exploded. Rosie's mouth was open in a silent scream as she came.

Mika forced her fingers as far as she could into her pussy and tight ass. Juice squirted from Rosie's pussy in a delicate arch. It splashed and pumped onto Mika's body hotly. Mika opened her mouth to catch some of Rosie's sweet nectar. Rosie watched in fascination as she ejaculated all over Mika.

When she finished cumming, Mika slid on top of her and kissed her gently. Rosie felt the rush of her cum from Mika's mouth. It was erotic and dirty. Both women continued to kiss and swap her juices until Rosie finally swallowed it. Rosie's body trembled lightly as they simply held each other for at least a half hour. Rosie couldn't wait until later when she would have the chance to fuck Mika in return.

9 CUSTOMER SERVICE

Making a Play

Belinda Carmichael smiled sweetly. Today was one of the worst days she had had for a while at the bank. The customers were rude and absurdly demanding. Her only recourse was an application she submitted earlier in the week. She had worked a teller window for three years and was done. Belinda loved the bank and didn't want to leave, but if she didn't get the account executive job she applied for, she'd most likely quit.

"Sir," she said nicely to the customer at her window. "You'll need to correct your deposit slips."

"I've waited in line for nearly an hour

and you want me to do what?" the jerk in front of her mouthed off.

"I'm sorry," she tried to explain, "but your slips don't add up to the check you've given me. See?"

Belinda kindly pointed out the customer's mistake. She leaned forward as if to get a better look at the slips and check and hoped the man would take notice. When the customer didn't follow suit, she looked up at him. He just stood there with a big smile. She glanced down for a moment, then straightened herself.

"What a pig," she thought to herself.

She caught him looking down at her blouse and he did nothing to avert his eyes afterward. She felt bad for a moment. Who could blame him? Belinda was a very sexy African-American woman. She had a body to die for. Her hips were the kind any man would love to grab a hold of and fuck her silly. Of course, her customer wasn't looking at her hips.

He was staring down her light, loose blouse at her magnificently large chocolate breasts. Belinda was sure most of the men that worked in the bank fantasized about her tits. They were large and soft and completely natural. No man in his right mind wouldn't fantasize about burying his face between them or squeezing them around his cock and tit fucking her.

That was one of her favorite things.

Belinda loved looking down at a nice hard dick pumping between her ebony mounds. She loved watching in anticipation of him shooting his spunk all over her chest and neck. She didn't know why; she just did. She had wondered if she harbored some kind of passion for porn, as she had a nice collection at home.

She wasn't into a guy blowing his wad all over a woman's stomach or covering her face with his jizz. She detested the "creampie" scenes, too. But there was nothing sexier than when a man shot his cum all over a woman's tits and neck. She could masturbate for an hour without cumming, but the moment she saw that, she came instantly.

Belinda was finally finished with her customer and she left her window for a moment to do some banking things. When she returned, he was standing there. He was Mr. Chance Laggo, a wealthy, white businessman with the looks of Adonis. Whenever she saw him, Belinda's heart would race and her pussy would drip. She wanted him badly but could never scrape up the courage to talk to him much.

"Good afternoon, Mr. Laggo," she greeted him as she tapped on her computer.

"Afternoon, Belinda," Chance replied.

He had smoothness that took her breath away. His deep voice sent shivers up and down her spine, and Belinda was sure he'd get a good look at her hardening nipples if it weren't for the blazer she was wearing. Chance watched her with his piercing bluish eyes. She felt completely naked beneath his gaze. Belinda wanted to be completely naked against his body: that was for sure.

Today she decided to be bold. It was now or never. So Belinda excused herself to take Chance's paperwork to the back. She processed the transfer and printed his receipt. This time, however, when she put his paperwork back in the envelope, she slipped a little note in with her name and telephone number.

She was trembling when she returned and completed the exchange. Mr. Laggo gave her his usual debonair smile and bid her good day. As she watched him leave, she licked her lips and hoped he'd call. She had a shot, right?

Just a Taste

A few weeks went by and Chance didn't call. In fact, Belinda hadn't seen the suave businessman at all in the bank. She began to think maybe she offended him. At least he hadn't complained to the branch manager or she'd be out on the curb. Then again, he could just be away on business. Regardless, he hadn't called.

"Morning, Belinda," Chance greeted her.

She was startled and turned around to look at him. Belinda hadn't heard anyone at her window.

"Oh, I'm sorry," she apologized for not paying more attention. "Good morning, Mr. Laggo."

"That's quite alright," he assured her smoothly.

She smiled sweetly. He was looking more handsome than usual, and again the sinful thoughts crept into her head. She pictured herself bouncing up and down on his gorgeous cock with her pillowy tits bouncing all over. Belinda could feel the heat stirring in her ebony quim and realized she was only wearing a sheer blouse. She was afraid to glance down. For sure her nipples were hard and quite visible through her white lace bra and thin shirt.

"How can I help you today?" she asked politely to recover from her hidden desire.

"I need my safety deposit box," he told her.

Belinda offered to place him on the customer service list since her duties as a teller didn't normally include giving customers access to their safety deposit boxes. Chance explained that the list was rather long for service and he was hoping she'd be able to help him. At first she was a bit apprehensive, but when he flashed his pearly whites, she was convinced to help him.

After retrieving his box, Belinda led Mr. Laggo to the privacy room. She closed the door behind them and went to put the bank's key in the lock. Suddenly Chance reached around and grabbed her tits. At first she was surprised and resisted reflexively, but when he pulled her back against him, she went nearly as limp as a doll. She submitted herself to him completely.

"So is this what you've been waiting for?" Chance whispered softly.

His warm breath heated her soft, smooth neck and she shivered. Belinda simply nodded her response while Chance squeezed and fondled her large chocolate tits. His strong hands felt wonderful on her body and she moaned her delight. Belinda couldn't believe this was actually happening.

Her eyes were closed while she let Chance have his way with her. She felt his hands move to her hips. He pulled up her skirt and nearly ripped her white lacy panties off. He roughly bent her over and Belinda groaned at the feeling of his thick hard cock pressing against her wet chocolate pussy. She trembled lightly in anticipation.

Suddenly Belinda screamed in lustful euphoria. Chance stuffed the entire length of his pulsating cock into her. Belinda held onto the edge of the table with white knuckles as Chance drilled her tight creamy pussy fast and hard. He placed a hand on the back of her neck and held her down as he fucked her madly. She could already feel the pressure building from her orgasm.

Belinda tried to move her deliciously large, round black ass to meet his relentless thrusts, but he had her pinned against the table. Even if she could move freely, there was no way she'd be able to keep up with his rhythm. It almost sounded as if he were beating her. His hips slapped against her ass in a deep, cupped echo.

She moaned faster and louder with each powerful thrust. She was on the verge of cumming and Chance knew that. He pulled his raging meat from her quivering pussy. Belinda groaned in contempt. She wanted him in her. She felt empty without his cock stuffed deep in her salivating cunt.

"On your knees," Chance commanded her smoothly.

Belinda obliged and knelt before him. She was amazed at his composure. He seemed just like the man who smiled at her at the teller window, not at all like someone who had just pounded the living daylights out of her. Belinda looked up at Chance submissively. His large cock pulsed just a few inches from her face.

"The blouse and bra," he commanded again.

Once again she obeyed, removing her blouse and bra. She could see the hunger in his eyes when she released her large ebony tits. Her nipples were hard and crowned one of the best sets of 36DDs Chance had ever seen. Belinda's eyes never strayed from his powerful gaze.

She knelt there patiently as Chance began stroking his cock. The expression on his face never changed. He didn't breathe harder. He didn't seem to get tired. He just stood over her and jerked himself off. Soon a tiny grunt came deep from Chance's throat and he came. His menacing cock showered her tits with his thick cum.

When he was done, Mr. Laggo stuffed his semi-flaccid dick back in his trousers and zipped his fly. He produced a cell phone from the breast pocket of his blazer and sat it on the desk. Then without another word, he left. Belinda looked around the room. She was feeling shocked, aroused, and vulnerable all at the same time. All she could do was get dressed, with Chance's cum slowly soaking into her bra, and go back to work. She nabbed the cell phone on her way out.

Bound and Blindfolded

Over the next few days, she worked as usual at the bank. Chance's cell phone was always next to her station and she constantly thought of that moment in the privacy room. Belinda thought he was clever. The privacy room is the only place in the entire bank that didn't have monitoring video cameras. Smart, very smart.

On Saturday the cell phone Chance had given her jingled. It was a simple text to tell her to go outside. When she did, a tall, slim man dressed as a chauffeur was standing next to a limousine. He nodded his head in greeting and held the door open for her. Belinda looked around briefly, then crawled inside. She was alone.

After a long drive, they arrived at a large luxurious house. A butler waited for her at the front door. He led her up to a bedroom and showed her in. He indicated to a wrapped box with a bow on it. The butler told her that Mr. Laggo would be home soon and she should change quickly. When she was done, she needed to press the little intercom button next to the bed.

Belinda nodded and the butler promptly left. She walked around the enormous bedroom for a moment, admiring the décor. Chance had great taste and the room reflected it. She looked at the box curiously before opening it. Inside was a rather expensive and elegant lingerie set. She smiled and quickly changed. When she was finished, she looked at herself in the mirror.

The icy blue color of the bra and panty set was a stark contrast to her ebony skin. Every piece seemed to accentuate her body. The small, silky thong panties were very sexy. She loved the way the back disappeared deeply between her bubbly, soft ass cheeks. The small patch on the front cut low in a "V" shape and barely covered her moistening pussy. Lucky for her, she had shaved it that morning.

The garter belt and thigh-high stockings made her legs and hips look simply hypnotic. She could imagine how she looked when she walked. The bra was different than anything she had worn before. It was half-cupped to gently lift her breasts and leave them mostly uncovered. She licked her fingers and teased her already-erect nipples.

After she admired herself for a few more minutes, she pressed the intercom button. She expected someone to answer her on the other end, but instead a woman came into the room. She was dressed in a skimpy French maid outfit and seemed very well mannered.

"Lie down on the bed please, Ma'am," the maid said.

Belinda gave her a puzzled look, but when the maid said nothing else, she did as she was told. The woman spent some time getting Belinda positioned just right, which seemed odd. Eventually Belinda was lying somewhat propped up on a slew of firm but comfortable pillows. She watched the maid reach into a drawer and pull out some pieces of cloth. They were icy blue to match her outfit.

The woman crawled onto the bed and straddled Belinda's lap. She delicately took one of her arms and stretched it out. When the maid began to tie her wrist to the bed's headboard, Belinda started to pull away. The woman's gaze held hers until she let the maid continue her work.

Belinda took a deep breath and exhaled slowly. She was very aware that the woman's heavy breasts were just inches from her face. She could smell the sweet perfume from her skin and couldn't help but stare at the maid's bountiful cleavage. When the maid was done, she looked down at Belinda and smiled.

"Mr. Laggo will be home soon," the woman said with a sensual tone in her voice. "Mr. Laggo is good, very good."

Belinda looked up at the woman in hunger. Her lips trembled and she could feel the wetness of her pussy creeping down her puffy lips and over her tight asshole. The maid bent down and kissed her softly on the lips. While she never imagined being attracted to another woman, Belinda hurriedly kissed the woman. Her body was on fire and she needed to be touched, even if it was the maid.

The maid broke the kiss and traced her lips down the side of Belinda's creamy neck. Belinda moaned softly and started to breathe harder. She couldn't wait for Chance to return. The woman circled her tongue around one of Belinda's hard, aching nipples and sucked it gently. She continued to do so until the Nubian was in a frenzy.

When the maid finished, she slipped a blindfold over Belinda's eyes and promptly left. Belinda was on fire. Her hips had a mind of their own and undulated with anticipation. Unable to touch herself, she squeezed her thighs together to put more pressure on her hungry pussy. She couldn't take it anymore and prayed Chance would arrive soon.

Belinda heard the bedroom door close with a resounding click. She flinched at the noise. She never heard the door open to begin with. Footsteps drew closer to the bed and Belinda felt her stomach knot with nervousness and anticipation. It was exciting and scary at the same time, but she was melting. Belinda had never been tied up or blindfolded before.

"Hello, Belinda," Mr. Laggo greeted her smoothly. "You look stunning. I hope you liked what I picked out for you."

"Yes," she replied with a soft, submissive voice. "Very much."

"Good," he said.

Belinda jumped slightly at the touch of something on her lips. Her chest heaved in deep breaths as she waited for it again. Something traced the outline of her lips and prodded at her mouth. It was too slender to be Chance's dick so she thought it was his finger. It was soft and smooth to the touch, but when she lashed her tongue at it, it withdrew.

"Do you like this?" he teased.

"Yes," Belinda replied breathlessly.

Again, she felt the touch and this time parted her lips slightly to receive it. The object pressed into her mouth slowly. It was long and smooth and not Mr. Laggo's finger. She couldn't figure out what it was, but she allowed him to move it in and out past her full, pouting lips. She sucked on the slender object gently, then moaned when it came to life in her mouth.

The vibrations made her entire body ache in desire. She had never felt or used a vibrator before, but she knew that's what she was sucking on. Slowly it moved in and out of her mouth, becoming slicker with her saliva each time her tongue wrapped around it.

Belinda felt it leave her mouth and trace along her lips. The tip moved across her lips, then left. She tensed a little as she felt it touch her neck and slowly run its length. Belinda felt it continue down and across her chest. Her pussy throbbed and she could smell the musky aroma of her flowing juices filling the room. She was very turned on now.

The vibrator continued its trek over her body. It moved dangerously close to one of her hard nipples and she inhaled sharply. She wanted to feel it on her nipple. She imagined how it would feel. When the wet plastic sex toy finally touched her nipple, she came. The pleasure that shot through her body, emanating from her nipple, made her convulse slightly. She moaned loudly as her orgasm engulfed her entire being and wrapped her in an exotic shroud bliss.

The vibrator lingered on her nipple for a moment longer until the waves of pleasure ebbed before continuing on. The slow course down was driving her insane. She knew where it was going and wanted it there now. She couldn't imagine how much more powerful the sensation of the vibrator would be on her tingling cunt. She felt a light tug on her panties and the cool bedroom air washed coolly over her exposed, dripping pussy.

Belinda arched her back and screamed

when the tip of the vibrator found her clit through her panties. The intensity of the pleasure blinded her brightly to the darkness she saw behind the blindfold. Points of white and gray and purple exploded across the darkness of the blindfold. Her thighs closed around the vibrator and her hips began to gyrate.

Her arms flexed against their bonds as she moaned erratically. She wanted Chance more than she wanted anything in the world. Belinda thought she had hit the ceiling that day at the bank in the privacy room, but that was nothing compared to the euphoria that was threatening to engulf her.

Chance increased the pleasure on her clit and slid the vibrator over it slowly. He moved the tip deeply through her pussy lips. Belinda lifted her ass off the bed repeatedly each time, trying to find the right angle to work it into her pussy. Chance denied her with each attempt.

The vibrations doubled as Chance clicked the control a notch. Belinda began bucking her hips wildly against the smooth plastic. She thrashed her head side to side and tugged hard at the ties that bound her wrists to the headboard. Her pussy was on fire and she was on the verge of climax.

Suddenly she felt the vibrator slide into her pussy. She grunted several times and came. Her pussy squeezed around the toy in a death grip. Her mouth was agape in a silent scream and her entire body tensed at the overwhelming sensation. Her juices flowed and flowed for what seemed like forever as the intense pleasure stabbed through every inch of her body.

When she was done, she collapsed in a heaving mess. She felt the vibrator slide from her used cunt and heard the vibrations stop. Belinda's head hung limply as she tried to recover from the most powerful orgasm she had ever had. She couldn't believe a woman could be taken to such heights, and this was only her second encounter with Mr. Laggo.

"You were beautiful," Chance whispered in her ear before placing a kiss on top of her head.

The next sound she heard was that of his fading footsteps and the door closing behind him. Belinda was alone and spent and still tied to the bed. She closed her eyes behind the blindfold and wondered what sort of sinful act he had in store for her next. She slowly drifted off to sleep for a much needed rest.

10 SMOKING THE BEAR

Making Due

Rose Schilling groaned as she rolled over in her little tent. Her firm, fit, 23-year-old body screamed at her in defiance for making it sleep on the cold, hard ground. It wasn't her body's fault she'd forgotten the air mattress. It wasn't her body's fault she didn't pay attention to the size tent when she bought it before travelling across the state to go camping in the mountains. So this morning it was getting some payback.

"You okay in there?" a voice called from outside the tent.

It sounded like her friend Kami, but she wasn't sure. It was hard to hear past the throbbing in her head. When she didn't answer, a smooth, sun-kissed face poked through the opening of her tiny shelter. It was Kami. She was smiling ear-to-ear and seemed as chipper as always. Rose's eyes opened to slits and she grimaced.

"Ready to go home yet, princess?" Kami teased her.

"Oh, can I leave?" Rose spat at her and pulled her sleeping bag up over her head.

Kami crawled into the cramped tent and gave the sleeping bag a good pull. Rose's eyes flung open in surprise and she lashed out and shoved her friend. Kami started giggling and fought to prevent Rose from covering herself up again.

"What the hell?" Kami laughed her ass off. "Why in the world would you wear something like that? Here?"

Rose was wearing a see-through babydoll with little bows and spaghetti straps. Her perky tits were very visible through the thin fabric and her nipples were hard as rocks. Kami reached out and pinched one and said something about how they must be frozen solid.

"Why not?" Rose frowned, wrenched the bag's flap away from her friend, and covered herself up.

"Because it's thirty degrees outside?" Kami chided and gave her that Are you stupid? Look.

Rose wasn't exactly stupid. She was actually rather intelligent. She just lived a life that included tropical islands and beaches. Her family had money so she never had to do without. Her idea of roughing it was flying commercial first-class instead of jet-setting in her father's private jet. So coming to the mountains was quite a change and one she wasn't enjoying.

"You could have warned me, Kam!" Rose pouted.

"Ummm," Kami teased. "What part of mountains sounds warm?"

"Just shoo!" she said and shoved Kami out of the tent by the face.

"There's coffee when you can get up, luv," Kami hollered.

Rose threw a sock at the little flap then just lay there. She decided she was out of her mind. She thought they'd be going to some fancy mountainside resort, not camping in the middle of woods at some campground with a communal shower and port-a-potty. Already she wasn't really enjoying it and they hadn't even been there a day.

Kami, her best friend in college, got the great idea of hiking the outdoors and somehow convinced her and several other friends to go. She decided to go partly because it was something she had never done before. But the main reason was to show all of her and Kami's "non-rich" friends that she wasn't some snot-nosed prissy and could slum it with the best of them. Maybe she was wrong.

She twisted around and flung the sleeping bag's flap off of her. Aside from not being very warm at all, she didn't see the problem with wearing her babydoll. In fact, she thought it was rather sexy. The rough, heavy lining of the sleeping bag felt good rubbing against the sheer lace of the outfit. It made her feel like her entire body was being caressed by some hidden lover; that was ultimately the reason her nipples were hard, not the cold.

The warmth of Kami's touch on her nipple still burned. Sinuous tendrils of pleasure snaked through her medium-sized breast. Rose didn't know why that playful pinch stirred the heat inside of her so much, but it did. Maybe it was the thought of being in the outdoors. Maybe it was the ruggedness of the nature around them and the idea of having beautiful sex in it somehow made the place less daunting.

Whatever the reason was, Rose was horny now thanks to her silly friend. She looked at her watch; it wasn't even seven. If she remembered correctly, they had a guided hike at nine, which gave her plenty of time to indulge in a little playtime before making an appearance around the campfire. So she did.

Rose covered up with the sleeping bag

and worked her babydoll off. She'd have to get undressed anyway to change into her hiking clothes. The plaid, wool lining felt enticing against her succulent skin and she let her hands maneuver where they wanted. She didn't go right for her pussy. Rose loved foreplay, especially when she was alone. No, she moved her hands along the tops of her thighs, keeping her legs closed playfully.

She closed her eyes and started to fantasize. Her hands slowly travelled along her body, lovingly caressing her supple skin. Rose burned with desire and stifled a moan when she cupped her breasts and began squeezing them. She kept reminding herself she was in a little tent that offered virtually no insulation against sound.

Rose's body ached from the pleasure that ran through her being. With each squeeze of her breasts and each tease of her rock hard nipples, she could feel her pussy growing wetter and wetter. She could already smell the musk of her juices; she adored the smell and reveled at the taste.

Rose knew so many women who refused to taste themselves. She couldn't imagine not doing that. Rose often wondered what they did in the heat of passion after their man got done eating them out and wanted to kiss them with their pussy juice all over his lips and mouth. Did they tell him to wipe it off? Not kiss him? Or was it different than when knowingly sucking their juices off of their fingers?

The momentary reflection ended with her doing just that. She slid her juiced fingers into her mouth and sucked on them gently. She moaned silently at the taste of her pussy on her tongue. It was very erotic, though she couldn't imagine tasting another woman.

"Hey princess!" Kami shouted from around the campfire.

Rose tried to ignore her at least until she came, which wasn't very far off. She had her fingers shoved in her mouth as far as she could, nearly gagging herself, while she quietly fingered her hungry pussy. Rose closed her eyes and concentrated, trying to block out her friend.

"Rose!" Kami shouted as she ducked her head inside the tent.

Rose jumped and glared at her friend with quite a bit of embarrassment in her face. Kami quickly looked away and started to giggle. She slowly turned to look at Rose then slowly climbed into the tiny tent.

"What the fuck, woman?" Kami whispered.

"What?" Rose tried to act innocent.

"What do you mean, 'what'?" Kami teased her. "I saw you!"

"I have no idea what you're talking about," Rose parried.

"You were fingering yourself!" Kami said a little louder and surprised Rose by tugging the sleeping bag open a bit. Rose's naked tit flashed into view momentarily before she covered up.

"Get the hell out," she shoved at Kami.

"No," Kami fended Rose off. "Wait!"

"What?"

"You think you're horny now," Kami whispered. "Get your wet ass out by the fire. The guide is here and he is one fine piece of man!"

Now that is something that Rose could use. Sexy images of her and this guide screwing every which way in the mountains began to flood her mind. Since she was so rudely interrupted halfway to a much-needed orgasm, she could really go for a cock in her burning pussy.

Ranger Jones

Five minutes later, Kami and Rose appeared from the little pup tent and stood by the fire. Rose eyed the ranger up and down and definitely agreed with her friend's assessment. Ranger Jones, his name badge just said Jones, was tall with broad shoulders and very muscular arms. His flat-topped hair had a hint of gray to it and he looked just like the Marlboro man in a green Forestry uniform.

"So who do we have here?" Ranger Jones nodded in Rose's direction. "City gal, I take it?"

Their group of friends snickered and gave Rose a knowing look. City gal didn't even start to describe her. Ranger Jones gave her a smile. His chiseled jaw and bright, straight teeth gave him that down-to-earth-good-guy-who-could-screw-me-anytime look to her. Rose was going to bed him, mountains or not.

Over the next few days, she lingered around him a lot. She asked questions and seemed genuinely interested in the sights they saw and facts they learned. Her charms seemed to be working on him because he always seemed to stare at her whenever she was around. Wearing tiny little shorts and showing some smooth, creamy thigh probably helped her cause.

"So?" Kami asked her the night before their last of the trip.

"So what?" Rose asked back as they sipped coffee and enjoyed the heat of the fire.

"Have you hooked up with Jones yet?"

Rose frowned and shook her head. Despite all her best flirting, Ranger Jones just didn't seem interested. There was only one night left and she was getting desperate. Then an idea struck her like a hammer. She knew exactly how to get this mountain man in the sack. After all, what dashing, brave, hunky ranger wouldn't help a beautiful damsel in distress? Rose smiled to herself and continued sip her coffee.

The next morning, Rose was up before anyone else. She was dressed and already had a fire going by the time Ranger Jones did his usual morning drive-by. Rose stood up and waved politely at him as he slow-rolled by. Jones eased his truck to a halt and Rose took a few steps his direction before slipping and falling to the ground.

Ranger Jones was beside her in a flash. She made like she was okay and tried to stand but complained of an intense pain in her ankle. Her knight in shining armor had her shoe and sock off and was examining her ankle. Rose shivered at his gentle touch and quickly hid her enormous smile behind a frown when he glanced at her.

"It doesn't seem to be swelling," Jones said as he caressed the smooth skin of her ankle.

"It feels tight and warm," she said in a very submissive tone. "Do you think it's broken?"

"Nah," he chuckled. "Probably sprained."

She pouted and looked down at the ground. Jones stuffed her sock in the shoe and tossed it into the bed of his truck. He took her in his massive arms and carried her toward his pickup. Rose wrapped her arms around her hero's neck and gazed at him.

"Let's get you to the station," he said. "I'll wrap it up but you better stay off of it just to be safe."

The Bear

The whole time they drove, Rose sat quietly in the passenger side of the truck. She faked a groan here and there when they hit a bump in the road. Finally, they arrived at the little station and Jones carried her inside. He sat her down on the couch and disappeared to get his first aid kit.

When Jones returned, Rose was kneeling on the floor completely naked. She looked at him with hungry eyes and held her wrists together in front of her. Jones smiled and eyed her up and down. She was sure he would have tripped over his tongue had he taken a step forward at that very moment. The rugged guide pulled a flexible bandage wrap from the first aid kit and wrapped it snuggly around her wrists.

Rose reached out and started to rub her hands over his crotch. Jones closed his eyes and groaned. His enormous cock started to strain against his shorts, begging to be free. She leaned forward, nibbled at his thick shaft through the fabric on his shorts, and moaned. It felt entirely too big for her but the look in the ranger's eyes told her she'd gone too far to stop now.

She melted at the wild look in his eyes. She pictured him taking her every which way, whether she liked it or not. Rose hoped he was rough. With his solid build and massive stature, she was sure he'd manhandle her until he got what he wanted. Oddly enough, it was the same thing she wanted.

Jones reached down, unbuckled his belt, and soon kicked his shorts across the small room. His monstrous cock stuck straight out, completely hard, and extended for what seemed like a mile. She had never seen a dick so large before and was rightly intimidated. When she didn't reach for it immediately, he grabbed her by the hair and tugged her forward.

Jones slapped her across the face with his massive cock. The slap echoed through the small station and Rose jumped at the solidness of his meat. He shoved the head of his cock into her mouth and she had no choice but to accept it. Jones held the back of her head tightly and fucked her mouth violently. She could feel the head of his cock stab the back of her throat with each thrust. Rose did her best to time her swallows but the man was too fast.

She begged through her moans for him to stop, which seemed to only urge Jones on more. He stuffed his angry cock into her mouth and down her throat faster and harder. Tears ran down Rose's face and her chest heaved with gulping breaths. She began to wonder if she had made a mistake. Rose felt dirty and violated, just the way she wanted.

Jones was grunting and growling like a bear. His eyes were closed tight and Rose could see the strain and intense concentration on his face. Suddenly her Boy Scout hero grabbed her and forced her onto the couch. He had her legs up with her ankles resting on his shoulders and his enormous, throbbing cock buried into her soaking wet cunt in a matter of seconds.

Rose reached over her head and held onto the back of the couch with her bound hands. Her breasts bounced wildly as Ranger Jones fucked the living daylights out of her. His hips made a loud, echoing slap against her ass and thighs with each powerful thrust. Rose couldn't believe she was able to take the girth of his massive dick without the slightest pain. She was hotter and wetter than she had ever been in her life.

She started screaming at the top of her lungs as her orgasm quickly invaded her body. Jones fucked her like a wild beast, fast and hard with no regard to her needs. He seemed completely oblivious that she was in her throes of cumming and was intent to satisfy his own carnal desires. All of that was completely okay with Rose. The euphoria of her powerful orgasm blinded her to the world. All she felt was the pleasure exploding throughout her body.

Jones started to growl viciously and pulled his dick from her gaping cunt. He crawled through her legs and straddled her. He jerked his cock hard and came. His thick jizz exploded from his cockhead and rained all over her face and chest. Rose opened her mouth wide and jerked her head around to try and catch some inside.

When they were done, Mr. Charming rubbed his cum all over her face with his throbbing cockhead and smiled. Rose's chest heaved as she tried to catch her breath. Their eyes locked for a moment before the ranger stuffed his meat away and left. He had a hike to guide. Rose just lay there alone, broken and stunned, and fully satisfied at the savageness of their sex.

She couldn't wait for him to return.

11 A IS FOR AIDE

Rescheduled

"Professor Grant will be with you in a moment," the secretary said after hanging up her phone.

Mindy Honeycutt thanked the woman and sat down to wait. The chair was plain and not very comfortable. It reminded her of the kind you'd find in a doctor's waiting room. It looked nice, not very extravagant, but mostly purchased because it was inexpensive. It wobbled a little, too.

Mindy was Professor Todd Grant's chemistry aide. At twenty-six, she was barely working on her Master's degree and had missed out on several opportunities to work closely with him. Several faculty members pegged Grant to be the university's next science dean, which made aide positions a very hot commodity.

She had no doubt why she was chosen. It obviously wasn't for her brains. Mindy was intelligent, that was for sure, but she'd only accomplished her bachelor's degree after eight years, although she'd taken two years off during that timeframe.

Mindy was an absolute stunner. She was slender and tall. Her hips weren't as curvaceous as she'd like, but her breasts made up for that shortcoming. When she pulled her long, raven black hair up and donned her round-framed glasses, she had that naughty teacher, closet-nympho librarian look. In other words, Professor Grant chose her simply because she was the most delicious piece of eye candy who had applied.

For the past year they worked well together, but in the recent months, she noticed he'd look at her body more often. She knew he was having marital problems, but even if he wasn't, she didn't blame him for sneaking a peek now and then. She did. She loved staring at herself in the mirror, nude or in just her bra and panties. Mindy thought she was hot; apparently so did the good professor.

"You can go in now, dear," the aged woman behind the desk informed her.

"Thank you," Mindy said and collected her things.

Professor Grant looked at her over the rim of his glasses when she walked in. She noticed his eyes paused for a moment before meeting hers. She wore a rather short skirt today and was sure he took that moment to drink in the sight of her smooth, shapely legs. He sat his papers down and stretched back in his chair.

"Good afternoon, Mindy," he greeted her.

There was something about his voice that made her melt. It was firm and confident. Not overly deep, it was a manly voice nonetheless. Couple that with a chiseled face, the sexy graying on his sideburns and his piercing brown eyes, and Professor Grant could have been the man of her dreams. If only he was twenty years younger, she'd definitely make a play on hm.

"Afternoon, Professor," she returned politely and sat down in the lavish chair across from him at the desk.

Something stirred inside of her today. It was innocent enough but something made her tingle inside. Sure, she was attracted to him, but she found herself attracted to most men lately. Her sex life was pretty much nonexistent, unless you counted her self-gratification when she was alone in her apartment.

She took out her planner and relaxed against the comfortable, high back of the leather chair. She slowly crossed her legs and gently tugged at the hem of her skirt. It was stretched as far toward her knees as it would go, but couldn't hurt to try. With her pen in hand, she waited for him to start their discussion.

"I'm afraid we're going to have to reschedule our meeting for tonight," he said as he shuffled through his papers.

"Okay," she simply replied and thought for a moment. "Do you want me to start grading the mid-terms at least? I don't mind."

Her sweet smiled seemed to warm him a little and he returned the gesture. "No, that's fine. They are spraying my office in a little while and, well, it's like a warzone at home. So enjoy your weekend and hopefully by class on Monday I'll have found a time we can get together again."

"If that's all that we're cancelling for, why don't we meet at my apartment?" Mindy offered somewhat nervously. It's not like she was inviting him to her place to get it on, but she would definitely understand his apprehension to meeting at her apartment.

"That's not necessary," Professor Grant, replied though he was touched by the offer.

"Come on," she said, getting a little bolder. She really wanted to see what he was like outside of the office, even if they were still going to be working.

"No, really," he argued lightly. "It can wait."

"I know it can wait," she argued back. "But then we'd have to cram to get everything graded and review the research papers."

They stared at each other for a moment. It was like a game of chess. They were testing the each other while maneuvering for an advantage. He was playing the 'I'm the boss' game; she wasn't sure what game she was playing. Finally, she decided to break the stalemate.

"Tell you what," she said as she scribbled something on a piece of paper. "Be there at six. I'll make us a little dinner and we'll get the research papers done. I'll have Cathy send everything over and I'll take care of the mid-terms over the weekend."

Before he could answer, she leaned forward and placed the paper with her address on his desk. She made sure to give him a good view of her breasts down her blouse. She wasn't wearing a bra today. Then after she knew he'd had his fill, she promptly left. Of course, she gave her ass that little extra wiggle on the way out. As the office door closed behind her, she smiled. Maybe she was being selfish, but she didn't want to cram all of that work into a Monday afternoon.

Setting the Hook

Mindy hummed to herself as she cleaned her apartment. She hadn't really thought of Professor Grant in a sexual manner, but the glimpse of desire she caught in his eye this afternoon got her thinking. She needed a man. It'd been nearly a year since her last tumble between the sheets. It was quite obvious that Professor Grant, Todd, hadn't had a piece of ass for a lot longer than that.

Conveniently for her, she'd be having him over soon. She decided to wait and see where the evening went. When Professor Grant arrived, he was greeted by a stunning sight. Mindy was wearing tiny, tiny sweat shorts and a tight tank top that exposed her delicious midsection. Mindy's nipples were already hard and they were straining very visibly against the fabric of her top. She decided to exclude panties and bra from her attire. This was her home, after all, and she felt like being comfortable while they worked. Right?

Professor Grant stammered his greeting. Mindy could see the hunger in his eyes. He was hooked and she knew it. She politely invited him in and took his briefcase and armful of papers. She led him into the comfortable living room, where she slowly placed his items on the table. She made sure to bend at the hips and take her time arranging the articles.

Mindy thought she heard him inhale sharply at the inviting site of her tight, round ass, especially since her shorts rode up a bit between her cheeks.

Professor Grant, or Todd as she was referring to him now, sat on the couch and gratefully accepted an offer of some wine. Mindy disappeared into her kitchen to fetch their drinks. She gazed at her reflection on the surface of the wine in Todd's glass. She took a few breaths to convince herself this was what she wanted.

She envisioned her plan of seduction in her head. It was like something out of a movie, but she was sure it would be very effective. She had been extremely horny since she decided what she was going to do. Mindy was already very wet. She checked several times and a few of those times, she let her fingers linger a little longer than they should have. Her fingertips brushed over her nipples lightly, refreshing them to a highly aroused state before taking his glass and returning to the good professor.

When she returned to Todd, she had completely lost focus of her ingenious plan. She panicked inside and looked around fervently for help. She couldn't find it. Mindy decided that she might as well be upfront about her intensions.

The Meeting

She stood in front of him for a moment to let him bask in her hotness. Mindy offered the glass of wine to him and when he took the glass, she didn't let go. Todd's eyes shifted from the wine to her face to match her gaze. Mindy straddled him and eased onto his lap.

Their lips met in a fury of passion and need and they kissed urgently. Their tongues searched for the other excitedly. Their hands were all over each other as if they were distant lovers, meeting for the first time. In a way they were, but neither seemed to care. They just kissed hungrily.

Todd's hands moved down to her ass and squeezed her firm cheeks while she cast off his tie and unbuttoned his shirt. Mindy ground her hips into his crotch and could feel the hardness of his dick through the thin fabric that separated them. They continued to kiss as Todd fumbled to rip off his shirt after she unbuttoned it.

The Professor was very muscular for being an older man. His chest was tight and his broad shoulders were cut enough to see the power in them. Mindy broke from him long enough to lift off her tank top. Todd's chest felt wonderful against her soft, spongy breasts as she pressed her body against his. The heat between them rose as they continued to kiss, threatening to engulf them in an inferno of passion.

It was obvious to her that she needed him just as much as he needed her. To Mindy, it felt like they were distant lovers finally together to share a virgin moment of passion. As rushed as they were, their touching was tender yet determined. The passion in their kissing was gentle yet feverish. The feeling was overwhelming.

Mindy's desire built to a nearly unbearable level. She needed to have Todd. She needed to feel him inside of her. Mindy slid off his lap and dropped her shorts. Todd's eyes were glued on her the entire time as if he were marveling at the most precious creation ever placed on the earth. She unbuckled his trousers and together they worked them and his boxers off. Todd's magnificent, throbbing cock bounced into her sight and pulsed with passion.

She crawled back onto his lap and started kissing him deeply again. They slurped at each other's tongues gently as the pressure between them built. Mindy ground her hips into him, sliding her dripping pussy along Todd's pulsating cock. Todd groaned into her mouth with each movement of her hips. He pulled her up and craned his neck to sucked one of her hard nipples between his lips.

Mindy cried out in ecstasy as he nipped at her taut, sensitive nipple. Hot pleasure sparked through her body and spurred her hips to move faster over his raging shaft. It felt wonderful and the lust grappled at her pussy. She lifted herself off his lap enough to guide his glistening mushroomed head to her waiting quim. Mindy ran the head of his cock through her gaping lips from her juicy entrance to her clit and back.

She shuddered from the sensation of his glans moving deeply through her pussy. Then in one smooth motion, she pierced her slit and forced herself down on him completely. Mindy froze for a moment at the sensation of being completely filled with the professor's beautiful cock.

Mindy gazed lovingly down at Todd. Her fingers grazed gently through the curly hair on his chest as she started to move her hips gently to and fro. His cock slid easily in and out of her with each rock of her hips. She moved slowly but determinedly. She didn't want to rush, yet. Her beautiful breasts swayed gently as she rocked on his lap.

She picked up her speed a little and felt when Todd's masculine hands grabbed her hips. He massaged her hips and thighs gently as she moved. It was an incredible feeling. No, it was more than that. It was the most incredible feeling she had ever had with another human being, besides the waitress she bedded once when she was attending a community college.

Todd's hips started to gyrate to her rhythm. The sensuousness was overwhelming and was threatening to drive her mad to the point of simply fucking his brains out. Beads of sweat began to roll down Mindy's forehead. Her hips moved faster and Todd's matched. Soon she was bouncing up and down in his lap wildly. Animalistic desires pushed her harder.

Mindy's tits bounced erratically as she impaled herself time and time again on Todd's throbbing cock. She could feel her first orgasm starting to build. Her pussy squeezed his glorious shaft with each bounce. Her head was tilted back and Todd held her arms to keep her steady. Their moans filled the apartment and drowned out the sound of everything around them.

"Oh God!" Mindy moaned over and over. "Yesssss... You have such a beautiful cock baby! Fuck my tight pussy good!"

Todd wrapped his strong arms around her and rolled over with his pulsating dick still buried deep in her gripping cunt. Mindy adjusted herself slightly on her back under his weight. Todd hooked her ankles over his shoulder and started to hammer her sweet pussy like a machine. She held on to the edge of the cushion as if her life depended on it.

Each massive thrust deep into her cavernous heat drove her closer to her orgasm. Mindy reached down and rubbed her fingers over her dripping pussy. She moved them over her lips and put pressure on the sides of Todd's massive dick with each thrust. Her hips moved wildly as he fucked her and she humped her clit with the palm of her hand. For a moment, she felt as if she were going to pass out from the intense pleasure.

Soon she felt his rock hard shaft start to grow bigger. Mindy knew he was about to fill her burning hole with his thick seed and she wanted nothing less. Todd wrapped his arms around her legs and held her tight as he started ramming his meat into her for the long stretch home. His moans turned into deep grunts and his eyes had a wild, lustful look in them.

Mindy rolled her clit between her fingers. Her moans rose in pitch as she was thrown headlong into an abyss of pleasure. Her pussy squeezed around Todd's cock as she came. He pumped her relentlessly, then climaxed. The feeling of his thick, salty cum drove her deeper into wicked euphoria. When they finished, they collapsed together in a tangled, sweaty mass.

Mindy thought to herself that she definitely needed to have the good professor over more often.

12 SEXTUAL PLEASURE

Steaming To Relax

Martha had come home from a hard day at work. She dropped her keys and purse on her bed and tossed her clothes wherever. On the drive home, she decided she needed to soak in a nice hot tub, and hopefully the drain of the day wouldn't seem so bad. She couldn't recall the last time she had such a horrible day. Her only saving grace had been Steve.

Steve was a coworker she had gotten to know over the past few weeks at Fitch & Stein Inc. She'd only been at the investment house for a couple of months, but she still felt like an outsider. Being an administrative assistant, or glorified secretary, for Mr. Fitch meant that she spent most of her day behind a desk or simply out of the office running errands. Everyone always seemed so uptight that trying to strike up a conversation with anyone was like beating a dead horse.

Then she met Steve, and her outlook at work changed. He was so free and lighthearted, with a little devil in him. Martha was hot, plain, and simple. She was young with medium-length blonde hair and the most piercing eyes in the world. Her breasts were round and soft and made her blouses moan with every movement. Martha guessed the thing she liked about Steve was he wasn't cliché.

Most men that would talk to her always came up with some sort of corny, typical pickup line. That wasn't Steve's game at all. He either was blatantly up-front or graced her with his naughty allusions. There were a number of days she had gone home with wet panties just from their brief conversations. Today was no different, except Steve was out of town, but he managed a devilish e-mail or text throughout the day that would put a smile on her face.

As Martha eased into the steaming hot tub of water, she remembered the last thing Steve had texted to her. She had mentioned something about stress or being overworked, and he replied he'd be more than happy to work her over if it made her feel better. Martha giggled briefly in the tub and then closed her eyes to relax. About five minutes into her soak, her cell phone jingled.

She grimaced and dried off her hand to see who it was. She learned that even when she wasn't at the office, she needed to keep her cell close by. Mr. Fitch had the extremely annoying habit of texting a list of things for her to do on the way into the office the next day. Martha tapped her phone and waited to see what list of errands Mr. Fitch had texted her today. To her surprise, it was Steve.

Steve D: Hey delicious!

Martha couldn't help but crack a smile. Even something as simple as that was enough to help chip away at the tension. She thought for a moment and then replied.

Martha: So I'm told. What's up?

Steve D: Hmmm... I'd like to judge for myself. Sup?

Martha: Nuttin' honey, just enjoying a hot tub of water. You?

Martha waited for Steve to reply with something from his repertoire, but nothing came. She was a little surprised at the silence. She waited a bit more, then tossed her phone aside. As much as she enjoyed Steve's distraction earlier, now wasn't the time. Martha wanted to relax. She needed to relax.

The heat from the water seemed to melt the tension from her body. She was in heaven. Martha shifted slightly and felt the water caress her skin for the first time since getting in the tub. It was smooth and soft and reminded her that the day was truly over and she was home. That wasn't the only thing the water did.

Martha moved her hands over her shoulders lightly. They felt so smooth in the water as she caressed her skin. She let her mind slip into a naughty fantasy and her body responded immediately. As her hands traveled slowly down her chest and over her soft breasts, her cell phone jingled again. Martha groaned in contempt for the jingle. Her silky smooth hands stopped just short of her hard nipples as she opened her eyes.

Martha stretched a bit to look at her phone to see who it was, but the screen had gone dark by then. She pouted and dried off her hand to nab her cell. She thumbed her phone and had a text waiting from Steve. She anxiously pulled up her text log to see what he had said.

Steve D: Sorry... was banging the maid.

Martha stifled a giggle. She loved his naughty sense of humor because she had no doubt that he could actually be banging the maid. She thought for a moment about an equally naughty response and then replied.

Martha: I hope you weren't too HARD on her. ;-)

Steve D: LMAO... you could say that! Still in the tub?

Martha: Of course!

Steve D: Mmmm... I just got a visual. Very nice.

Before Martha could respond again, Steve texted her something that piqued her interest. He had told her he wouldn't bother her anymore so she could enjoy her relaxation, but to text him when she was done. His only caveat was she was to be wearing just a robe and nothing else when she did.

Martha: kk... ttyl! :-*

Martha set her phone down and relaxed. By then, the water had cooled some, so she added a bit more steaming hot water. It was almost paradise. All she needed was a cabana boy fanning her, and it would be perfect. After a half hour or so of heated bliss, Martha felt completely refreshed and decided it was time to get out of the tub.

Out of the Pan

Martha eased out of the tub and grabbed her towel. The thick, soft cotton towel felt very sensual as she moved it over her body to dry off. The towel felt like a gentle lover caressing every curve of her body, and it felt wonderful. The fast pace of her lifestyle and the demands of her job left her with very little free time to pursue a relationship. What it boiled down to was the fact that Martha hadn't been laid in months.

Martha decided that enough was enough. After spending a little too long drying her sensitive nipples and tingling nether region, she thought she should just get dressed and save her self-pleasure for later. Besides, she was getting hungry.

After dinner, she settled in on her couch to watch television. Martha glanced at her cell phone now and then and toyed with the idea of texting Steve. She was intrigued by the direction Steve could go with his text, but at the same time, she felt a bit embarrassed. Was he just being his devilish self or was he fishing for more? Martha wasn't sure she was ready to find out.

As the movie dragged on, she found herself drifting back to her bath and the sinful touching that almost was until Steve had interrupted her. More than a few times, she had caught herself gently massaging one of her breasts. She looked down at her hard nipples straining against the silk of her camisole. The sight of their hardened peaks outlined by the off-white fabric was intoxicating. Martha felt her insides stir with mischief and decided to retire to her soft, comfortable bed.

As she snatched up her cell phone, she remembered Steve's text. Martha took a deep breath and thumbed her phone on again. A few touches pulled up her texts and she reread the last one Steve sent: *Text me when you are finished... and only if you are wearing your robe and nothing else >:-).*

Feeling quite frisky, Martha decided she would comply. She slipped out of her silk camisole and eased her plain cotton panties down from her hips. She opted for her lacey robe rather than her warm cotton bathrobe. She pulled the silky fabric around her bare, succulent body and tied it at the waist. Martha slid sideways onto the bed and replied.

Martha: Okay, I'm finished.

She lay there and stared at her phone. She waited for a few minutes with baited breath. Martha couldn't remember exactly where Steve was, but hoped it wasn't too late at night. Her phone jingled. It was Steve.

Steve D: Good. What are you wearing?

Martha: Just my satin lace robe... and nothing else ;-)

Martha smiled with the smiley she sent to Steve. The anticipation was killing her. Apparently, she had thought about Steve more than she had thought. Maybe it wasn't exactly Steve she was wanting, but she was sure wondering what he was getting at.

Steve D: Great! What are you doing?

Martha: Laying here on my bed n texting you. Why? You planning something naughty?

Martha couldn't help but bait Steve. She wanted to know what he was up to. Simply put, she was horny and wanted to know whether or not to waste her time with Steve or have some fun alone before bed. Martha waited for Steve to respond again. After a few minutes, she grew impatient and texted him again. This time she added a bit of her own flare to the conversation.

Martha: Well? You should know that I'm HOT right now.

That got an immediate reaction from Steve.

Steve D: Really? How HOT are you?

Martha: Let's just say that my nipples are extremely hard and if I were wearing panties, they would prolly be soaked.

Martha smiled to herself. She was going to turn Steve's game against him, though she really was extremely hot. While she texted with Steve, she thought of some sexy things to say to him. Things like how she was touching herself and how she wished he were there with her. Martha wasn't immediately aware of just how much their brief sexting session was affecting her.

While she waited again, she brushed her hand down over one of her large, pillowy breasts. She teased her hardened nipple through the satin of her robe and inhaled sharply. Her cell phone jingled and she opened Steve's reply.

Steve D: Are you touching yourself?

Martha thought about telling him she was caressing her breast but decided against it. She wanted to see where he was going with this conversation.

Martha: No. Do you want me to?

Steve D: Yes. Though I wish it was me touching you. Why don't you massage your breasts through your robe and pretend it is me doing it?

Martha: Okay. >:-)

Into The Fire

Martha was more than happy to oblige. She sat her phone to the side and rolled onto her back. She felt the heat already stirring between her thighs and knew Steve would be naughty enough to satisfy her. Martha's hands slowly roamed over her chest. She grazed her fingertips along the outer curves of her breasts in tiny circles. Her touch felt amazing and sent goose bumps up and down her arms. She couldn't believe she was doing this.

Finally, Martha cupped her breasts fully with each hand and started to squeeze them gently. Her hard nipples strained harder against her satin robe with each loving caress. As Martha squeezed her breasts, she squeezed her fingers around and toward her sensitive nipples and then ended each time with a tug on her hard pebbles. She nibbled on her lower lip as the flames of desire burned hotter and hotter with each touch.

Martha: Mmmmmmm...

Steve D: Does it feel good?

Martha: Very good. Your hands feel soooo good on my soft tits.

Steve D: Yes, they do. Now take off your robe.

Martha did as she was told. As she slipped out of her sexy robe, Steve texted her another instruction. She cooed at his words. Martha gently sucked on her fingers until they dripped with her saliva. Then, as Steve instructed, she ran her moist fingers in circles around her aching nipples. She closed her eyes and pretended that her fingers were Steve's tongue. Her nipples folded then snapped into attention each time she ran her fingers over them. Martha's body jolted lightly from the shocks of pleasure radiating from her breasts.

Martha moistened her fingers again with her tongue and started to roll her erect nipples between them. Steve was so good. She could feel his lips circling her taut nipples and sucking on them gently. Martha moaned his name softly each time she pinched and squeezed her hard pebbles. Unconsciously her thighs started to rub together, increasing the pressure on her sizzling pussy. Indeed, Steve was even naughtier than she had first anticipated, and she loved it.

Martha: I love how you suck on my nipples. You are making my pussy soooo wet.

After she sent her text, she couldn't believe she actually said that. She knew she had a sexy streak in her too but never thought she'd be so blatant about it. She didn't care. If Steve could help her get off, then who was she to complain? If he were there with her right, then she'd happily fuck his brains out.

She closed her eyes and imagined Steve was there with her. She could see the broadness of his shoulders and how the muscles in his back rippled as he moved his sinful lips from breast to breast. Steve sucked and kissed the outsides of her breasts and slowly worked his way along their edges. Martha arched her back and moaned loudly as she felt his tongue lap at the soft, sexy crease beneath her right breast where it met her torso. She was on fire and Steve was intent on kindling that fire into a raging inferno.

Steve D: I want to taste your sweet

pussy now.

Martha quivered at the text. She couldn't imagine how much hotter Steve could make her, but she was more than willing to find out.

Martha: God yes! Please eat my hungry cunt now!

Steve D: Feel me spread your legs and caress the insides of your thighs.

Martha slowly spread her legs for her sexual lover. She raked her fingernails lightly along the insides of her thighs. She started at her knees and slowly worked toward her burning honey hole. Martha arched her back to Steve's touch. He knew just how to touch her to make her entire body tingle. Martha took a deep breath and proceeded to fulfill Steve's desires.

With one hand, she spread her juicy quim while she licked the index finger of the other. She licked and sucked on her finger until it dripped with her slimy saliva. Martha reached down and gently ran her wet, slick finger up and down between her spread folds. Her toes curled at the delicate touch of Steve's tongue on her lusting pussy.

Martha pressed her hand down and gently folded back her sensitive hood and exposed her throbbing clit. She ran the tip of her slender finer around her clit ever so slowly. Her hips began to move slightly against the waves of pleasure her naughty coworker had stirred inside of her. Martha was in heaven and had forgotten about her cell phone until it jingled. She blindly fumbled around to find it to see what dark desire Steve had sent her now.

Steve D: I want you to dip just the tip of your finger into your pussy. Get it nice and juicy, then rub it over your tight ass.

Martha nearly came at the thought of doing that. She had never been one who had gotten excited when a man wanted anal sex, but she was beyond her normal self now. She was like a hungry beast that desired to be pleasured in every way imaginable. So she did what she was commanded to do.

She slipped just the tip of her finger into her lusting hole. She struggled not to jam her finger inside and fuck herself furiously until she came. No. Her head swam with erotic images of Steve between her legs, using his tongue to stoke her desire until the world around her was gone and it was just the two of them left. She stirred her fingertip around her pussy's entrance for several moments and then did as she was told. She pressed her finger firmly against her tight asshole and smeared her cum in circles around her most taboo spot.

She pressed harder and felt the tightness slowly give way. She begged herself to do it. Steve never said she couldn't so she pressed even harder. Her ass ring stretched around her probing finger. As the first knuckle of her finger disappeared, she felt her pussy spasm and her body shuddered violently. Her orgasm shrouded her in an intense calm of pleasure and sin, and she refused to let it ebb quickly. She found her clit again with the other hand and rubbed it furiously.

Calming the Storm

Martha lifted one leg and pinned it under her arm for better access. She fingered her tight ass hard and fast. The palm of her hand slapped against her flaring pussy like a jackhammer with each thrust inside. Beads of sweat rolled from her heaving breasts, and her head whipped back and forth under the throes of ecstasy. The veil of her intense orgasm slowly slid from her body and left her hot but still fulfilled.

Martha: OMFG!!!! You just made me cum so hard!

Steve D: Mmmmmm... good... I take it you love playing with your ass?

Martha: Yes... I fingered my asshole for you like a slut.

Martha couldn't believe her eyes. She had just called herself a slut. Suddenly the world stopped as she realized the power Steve had over her. Her cell phone jingled again and this time she refused to look. Her body screamed for more and her pussy begged to be used badly, but she still couldn't bring herself to look. It jingled again but this time she looked.

Steve D: Good... you love being my nasty fucking slut, don't u?

Steve D: Don't you? Answer me now, u slutty whore!

Martha tried not to respond but she had lost all control of her will.

Martha: Yes. I love being your dirty slut.

Martha trembled slightly as she waited, and when his text came, she gasped. She was a healthy woman and had an above-average appetite for sex, but she didn't own any toys. She couldn't believe what he wanted to do, but it sounded so hot that she couldn't deny herself this final pleasure of the night.

She rummaged through her bathroom fervently until she found what she was looking for. It was a hairbrush with a very shapely handle. She decided it would do. Martha climbed back onto the bed and turned on the video recorder app on her cell. She got on her knees and eased herself down on the brush handle.

Its curved handle eased into her pussy easily and she moaned deeply at the feeling. It was hard and wide and was molded thickly in the middle. She spread her knees out further to put more pressure on the bristled head of the brush. She positioned her cell phone just right, then dropped forward onto her hands. Martha began moving her hips up and down, letting her pussy slide on and off the handle of the brush. The feeling was intense and she felt so dirty for doing this.

As her hips began to move faster, she imagined Steve's throbbing cock piercing her deeply over and over. She could feel her tits rubbing over his chiseled chest as she fucked him wildly. Martha's bedroom was full of moans and the smell of sex. Her juices dripped down the brush and soaked the thick comforter on her bed.

"Oh god, Steve!" Martha moaned loudly as she continued to impale herself deeply on his hard, beautiful cock. Her round, silky ass bobbed up and down as she fucked her pussy faster and faster, feeling another climax slowly approaching.

"Fuck me! Fuck me!" she screamed over and over, as she began trembling. Martha pumped her hips faster for her distant lover and moaned her every desire into her phone. Her legs began quivering, and she had to hold onto the brush with her hand to keep it from slipping away.

Martha dug her fingers into the comforter for dear life. Her hips flailed wildly as the first tremors of pleasure started rumbling deep in her pussy. She rode Steve's cock with every ounce of energy she had. Martha started to cum violently. The bed shook and one of the lamps was knocked from her nightstand. She arched her back and forced her hips down as hard and far as she could. The room swam with colors and her head spun quickly as if she were going to pass out.

When it was over, Martha collapsed and rolled onto her back. Her chest heaved behind heavy, ragged gasps as she tried to catch her breath. When she had recovered enough, she nabbed her cell phone and slowly slid the brush from her used slit. Martha looked into the camera mischievously and slid the brush handle past her lips and into her mouth. She devoured her pussy juice for Steve. Finally, she thumbed off the video recording app and nuzzled against her bed.

Martha drifted off to sleep with a satisfied smile on her lips. She couldn't wait to return the favor when Steve returned from his trip.

AUTHOR'S NOTE

Readers: I want to expand a few of the stories to see where the characters can be explored further. If there are any of the stories that you would like to read more about again, I'd love to hear from you!

Visit my blog at www.portisnewman.com

Join my newsletter for free exclusive previews
www.portisnewman.com/in

Follow me on Twitter at
www.twitter.com/portisnewman

Like my page on Facebook at
www.facebook.com/portisnewman

Discover my books at major ebook retailers everywhere.